The

Christmas Portrait
Surprise

Also by Phyllis Clark Nichols

THE FAMILY PORTRAIT SERIES
The Christmas Portrait – Book One
The Birthday Portrait – Book Two

THE ROCKWATER SUITE
Return of the Song – Book One
Freedom of the Song – Book Two
Ransom for a Song – Book Three
Christmas Wedding Song – Book Four
Searching for the Song – Book Five

Christmas at Grey Sage
Silent Days, Holy Night
Sacred Sense from a Second Look

The

Christmas Portrait
Surprise

The Family Portrait Series

—

Book Three

PHYLLIS CLARK NICHOLS

Southern
Stories
Publishing

THE CHRISTMAS PORTRAIT SURPRISE: Book #3 in The Family Portrait Series
Copyright © 2021 by Phyllis Clark Nichols

Published by Southern Stories Publishing

ISBN: 978-1-7369157-4-5 (paperback)
ISBN: 978-1-7369157-5-2 (ebook)
Print Edition

Cover art and design by Bill Nichols from an original oil painting by Bill Nichols

Dedication

For our daughters, our son-in-love,
and our three grandchildren

who carry on our family Christmas traditions and are making
new ones.

Christmas 2007

Kate

" *I* know you can't help it, and I do understand, but I can understand and still be sad and disappointed, can't I? I'll miss you. We'll all miss you, Henry. I love you."

Even as I spoke the words and ended the call, I wanted to chuck the phone across the room. Maybe toward the icy window in front of me. But something would get broken, and I'd have a mess to clean up. Then I'd have to file a report with Mr. Grebinger, the apartment manager, and he could top Granny Grace with his interrogation techniques. How would I explain a broken window and that my phone was four floors below on a frozen sidewalk? I could hear him grumbling now, complaining about Chicago winters and telling me how he was moving to Florida in eleven months.

But why this Christmas? Henry and I hadn't been home since our spring wedding, and this was to be our first Christmas to return to Cedar Falls as man and wife. Why did he have to be on assignment *this* Christmas—and in Africa of all places? I knew it wasn't his fault that he couldn't make it home, but I hated it.

It hadn't been Mama's fault she died, either, yet I hated that too. It seemed every Christmas since then had been like opening an old wound. I'd had more than my fair share of sad Christmases.

What's one more? Maybe I should just stay in Chicago and not inflict my misery on my family back in Kentucky.

I kicked off my shoes and walked across the thick pile of the Persian rug I had purchased in Morocco a few years ago on a trip with Daddy and Evie. Buying that rug was about the most impractical thing I've ever done, but Mama would have approved. Those warm reds and vibrant greens would have called to her just like they did to me. That blanket of a rug stretched wall to wall in our small apartment bedroom, and it always felt good to my feet.

I stood barefooted and stared out the window. The sky was dark gray, and the drifting snowflakes flickered in the light from Mike's Diner across the street. The chef made pots of soup that rivalled Granny Grace's, and Mike's stayed open late on frigid nights like this one just to accommodate the folks in the neighborhood.

Colored lights from Christmas trees flickered from apartment windows in the building next to the diner. I didn't even have a Christmas tree. No reason for one. Henry was still in Africa, and I was going home to Cedar Falls.

I preferred the nothingness of watching the snow accumulating on the window ledge, but the half-packed suitcase on the bed seemed to summon me. I walked back to the bed, slammed the suitcase shut, and slid it to the other side. Then I turned out the lamp on the bedside table and lay down. I'd learned at the age of ten it was best to cry in the dark. Crying in the light made my sadness more real, and if I cried in the dark, no one else had to know.

I was crying for past sad Christmases and for this one, which was turning out to be more of the same, when the phone rang. I sat up quickly, turned on the light, and wiped my face with my sweater sleeve as though I had been caught in some evil act I wanted no one to see. My phone had been ringing all day—clients trying to make that ever so important last appointment before Christmas. As a grief counselor, I knew Christmas opened wounds for grieving children. Emotional wounds like mine, with scars almost as visible as a surgical incision. In a way, losing someone was like the surgical removal of a vital organ or limb, and nothing was ever quite the same. You just learned to live with the difference.

I answered. "Hello, this is Dr. Harding."

"Kate, it's Granny. You busy?"

After Mama died, it was like Granny Grace developed some kind of sixth sense, always knowing when to call or show up. She'd lost her daughter when I lost Mama, so she mothered me and I daughtered her. It worked even after Daddy and Evie married. Evie was good that way, understanding I needed Granny Grace and Granny needed me.

"Kate, are you there? You okay? I asked if you were busy."

Granny had taught me never to lie, but I wasn't about to tell her I had been busy crying and feeling pity for myself. I cleared my voice. "A bit busy always. I'm looking at my half-packed bags."

"Well, get them packed full, sweet girl. We can't wait to see you and Henry. Susannah Hope and I've been doing the Christmas baking, and Evie's helping as best she can. Bless her heart, cookin' is still not her thing, but she does make up for it. She's a great cleaner-upper. She hasn't told us yet what her culinary contributions will be for the Christmas dinner table. And if she's true to her history, even if she tells us what it is, what's in her casserole dish will still be a surprise."

"Just please don't let her prepare the apples and sweet potatoes, or at least make her wait until I get home to help. She used olive oil and burned them to a crisp the last time."

I heard Granny chuckle. I needed to hear Granny's voice and that familiar chuckle tonight.

"Now you and Henry bring your warm clothes. Your Uncle Luke's planning his annual bonfire and ice skating after the Christmas Eve service. You know how Luke and Lisa are about getting on that pond at Christmas since that's where he proposed to her."

Just thinking about that icy pond made my bare toes curl. I searched the rug for my shoes. "You think they're getting a little old for that? They've been married what? Eighteen, nineteen years?"

"Nineteen, I think, but since they moved out there to my farmhouse, it's become one of those traditions every Christmas, and looks like the weather will be perfect this year. Oh, and tell Henry that Chesler's bringing his guitar, and we're expecting some carols out of those two. Must keep up these traditions. You know how we O'Donnells and Hardings are about our traditions."

I knew all too well about family traditions and the changes through the years. Those customs had grown sweeter and more valuable to me because I knew there would be more changes coming. That's why Henry's absence hurt so. No Henry in the family Christmas portrait this year. "Granny, about Henry."

"What about Henry? He's not sick, is he?"

"No, ma'am. He's not sick, but he won't be able to make it for Christmas. He hates it, but he can't get home."

Granny's momentary silence was worse than her chattering because it meant the inquisition was about to begin. "What do you mean he can't get home? Is he all right?"

"He's fine but still in Ethiopia on assignment and can't

get home until December twenty-ninth. He's really disappointed."

"Seems to me if he can get home on the twenty-ninth then he could get home on the twenty-third. So why can't he? What kind of folks is he working for that would keep him from his family at Christmas?"

I cleared my throat again, as though that would make my answer clearer to her. "Granny, you know he's on this big water project, and they're trying to finish up building some wells so that he doesn't have to return for a few months. Business doesn't work there like it works in Cedar Falls."

"Well, then, maybe you two should just move to Cedar Falls. There's plenty to do here to help poor folks and grieving, troubled children."

Granny had been singing this song since Henry and I became engaged. "We do know all about that, don't we, Granny? Maybe one of these days. But for now, Henry's work is changing the lives and the health of so many people around the globe."

"So you're coming home alone on your first Christmas as a married woman. Something wrong about that." Granny Grace paused. "Well, then, is he meeting you here to stay for New Year's Eve?"

"I don't think so. I'll just fly back to Chicago to meet him. We're thinking we need to start our own New Year's traditions."

"I'm getting too old for new traditions. My old ones suit me just fine. You belong here for Christmas, and so does Henry."

"I'll be there, Granny. You can count on me. I wouldn't miss all the family fun." I was relieved she wasn't looking at my face when I said that. For some reason, surprising images of Granny Grace sitting at her breakfast table explaining to me why she wouldn't be at home for Christmas flashed into my memory. Daddy and Evie had married in the autumn of 1991, three years after Mama died, and Granny Grace had just up and decided to take a trip that Christmas. "I'll be there on Saturday."

"Make sure you are, Katherine Joy. I don't know how many more Christmases I have left for this world."

"Now, Granny, you've been saying that for the last fifteen years, and you know I don't like it when you talk like that, and if you could see my face, you'd really know it." I paused. "You know, for some weird reason, I was just remembering that Christmas after Daddy and Evie married and you decided to take a road trip and spend Christmas with a group of friends from church. I remember being a bit angry with you. Do you remember that?"

Silence from Granny again. "I do seem to recall that stupid thing I did. Only I don't remember it quite like you do. Seems I remember you were a whole lot angry with me, and I was the one who got more than one good talking-to from my granddaughter about that."

"Um-huh. I remember that part too. You deserved it. You were just about to ruin our Christmas. That was the Christmas we made the family pact to be home for Christmas no matter what. Guess Henry's work didn't make that pledge." I sighed. "Thanks for the call, Granny. You always seem to know when I need to hear your voice. I'll see you in a couple of days."

"Make sure you do, sweet girl. Make sure you do. And remember to bring the Christmas tablecloth. Did you finish all the stitching? I'm dying to see what you did."

"It's here on the bed folded and waiting to be packed."

"I'll be so glad to see you, Kate. Love you, girl."

"Love you, too, Granny."

I put the phone on the table, grabbed a tissue from the

box on the nightstand, and went back to the window. The diner lights were still flashing, and snow was still falling. I was mesmerized by the scenes in the apartment windows across the street. Why didn't people close their blinds at night? I knew none of those people, but I knew so much about their lives. I didn't consider myself a voyeur, but Dr. Swanson, my major professor, would have been fascinated by Dr. Katherine Harding's interest in her neighbors. After a day of counseling and digging into people's stories and their lives in order to help them, I often found myself standing at my own bedroom window peering again into people's lives through their windows across the street.

With Henry away, our apartment was mostly silent except for the street noise below. For the last two weeks, the sounds of Christmas music had echoed through the whole apartment every evening. I'd wrapped Christmas packages. I'd baked cookies to take to the office and share with patients and staff. I'd written Christmas cards. I'd had such hopes for this being the best Christmas since Mama died. Now my hope lay somewhere deep within a well in Africa.

Tonight was silent and dark, and I felt like was on the outside looking in at everyone else's merry Christmas. In my aloneness, I stood safely behind partially opened curtains so that I couldn't be seen. The family on the second floor on the east side was a happy one. Three generations living in the same small apartment. Lots of activity, smiles, and conversations like the ones they were having around the table tonight. Probably Italian. Their Christmas tree was much too large for the space, but it was theirs, and it suited them.

The elderly lady next door lived alone, and her Italian neighbors invited her over for evening meals frequently, but not tonight. She watched television with a blanket around her legs and a steaming cup of something on the table next to her. A small, no doubt artificial, tree with tiny lights sat on a table in front of the window.

The couple above on the third floor—sophisticated, stylishly dressed—were drinking cocktails with their dinner guests. He spent hours on his computer at night while she read. Their apartment was glamorous, their holiday decorations silver, white, and gold. Granny would have laughed, and Mama would have hated it.

I had just enough information that I made up happy stories about each of them, but the truth was I knew they had their own stories that probably included some sad scenes. I wanted them to be happy. I wanted them to have the best Christmas ever. I wanted no one to feel the sadness I was feeling.

What would those people think of me, what stories would they concoct, if they were looking through my window this evening?

I didn't know how long I stood there. It felt like a life-time, several lifetimes, as I peered through their windows and into their lives. But finally, I closed the curtain and crossed the room to the bed. There lay the tablecloth. The O'Donnell Christmas tablecloth. I picked it up, gave it a good shake, and spread it over the bed. With smudges, stains, fingerprints, and dates and signatures in hand-stitching on the linen fabric, the Christmas tablecloth told the story of the O'Donnells and the Hardings for the last half a century.

I studied Mama's signatures from her childhood until her last Christmas. They were all fun, colorful, and creative and so different from Aunt Susannah Hope's, neat and straight and the same year after year. I looked at Chesler's bold letters, always green, and Daddy's and Grandpa's.

But there it sat in the left corner in brilliant red, signed and dated *1990*—the last year we'd used this tablecloth. I moved my index finger to trace Granny's curlicue handwriting. So many memories, but I remembered the Christmas when Granny went away. A flash, a memory of spreading that tablecloth on the Christmas dining table so many times, and I was hurled back to 1991, the Christmas when Granny Grace went away and the tablecloth became mine.

Chapter One

———— ♦ ————

Friday evening, December 13, 1991
Cedar Falls, Kentucky

Kate

$\mathcal{D}$ addy brought in all the boxes with the tree ornaments and stacked them on the stairs like he'd always done since I could remember. It was the plastic bin that held the treasures. Daddy's face changed when he lifted the lid. He handed Chesler his box of ornaments and tousled his red curls. "Here you go, sport. Take these to the living room." Then he picked up my box. "Kate, I believe these are yours."

I took the box and rubbed the red ribbon between my fingers. "What about Mama's box? Will we put those on the tree this year?" I couldn't imagine the tree without the ornaments Chesler and I had made for Mama, but this Christmas was different since Daddy had married Evie.

I'd been three when I made a bell out of a paper cup with glued-on sequins and gave it to Mama, and every Christmas after that I'd made an ornament for her just like she made one for Chesler and me. Chesler had only made two for her before Mama went to heaven, but Mama always kept them in a special box just like ours. The first ornaments on the tree always came from those three boxes that were kept in a separate plastic bin.

Daddy's face told me he didn't know what to say about Mama's ornaments. "It's okay, Daddy. I already thought about it, and me and Chesler each made an ornament for Evie this year. Chesler's giving them to her tonight. We didn't have a special box, but maybe we can get her one."

Daddy came straight at me with a hug. He held me close and whispered, "You bet we'll put your mama's ornaments on our tree. What in the world did I ever do to deserve a thoughtful daughter like you? I know Evie will love that you made one for her, and your mama would be so proud of you, Kate. I know this isn't easy. Christmas has been hard for all of us without your mama, and this one is a whole lot different. Evie's never had a family of her own for Christmas, and it's strange for her too." He kissed me right in the middle of my forehead where my red streak was.

Mama said it was an O'Donnell thing, that red streak. Grandpa had had it, and he'd passed it down to Mama, and me and Chesler got it too. It was a streak from my hairline to the top of my nose, and it turned red when I was upset or lying. That's why I could never tell a lie—because that streak spoke the truth, and it was probably red right now. I wasn't lying about anything, and it wasn't that I didn't like Evie and didn't want to do nice things for her, but I missed Mama so much, especially at Christmas. It just felt like I was lying.

Chesler came running. I don't think that boy ever learned to just walk. He was already in school and still running around everywhere in the house in his sock feet. "What about Mom's ornaments? You got 'em, Kate? I'm givin' 'em to her. You said I could." Chesler calls Evie "Mom," but Evie said it was okay that I wasn't ready to do that.

"Okay, Chesler, I have them. They're in a bag behind the chair next to the fireplace. And if you'll stop running around this house, you can give them to her."

Daddy said, "Another nickel, Ches. Go get it. You know what to do."

Evie had come up with an idea of a jar of nickels. Every time Chesler was called down for running in the house, he had to put a nickel from his allowance into this special jar. Evie didn't know yet that it wouldn't work. Chesler was too smart for that one. Just like when Mama tried to teach him the alphabet with flashcards and M&Ms. If he got the right answer, he got an M&M, but he had to give it back if he missed one. So Chesler started eating them as soon as he got one. He'd just spend his whole allowance so he wouldn't have any nickels to put in the jar.

Guess she'll figure that one out.

I took Mama's box out of the bin and put it on top of mine. "Oh, don't forget the big box of lights, Daddy. Remember, we put them up real good last year so they wouldn't be tangled."

Daddy grabbed the stack of boxes with all the ornaments and carried them to the living room. "We won't need the lights. Evie bought new ones."

I put my boxes on the piano stool. "But we didn't need new lights. We have lots of them."

"Evie wanted little white lights, not the colored bulbs we have." He put his boxes down on the floor and unstacked them and took the lids off.

"White ones? But we like the colored ones, the ones Mama—" I shushed when I saw Evie walk into the room carrying a bundle of lights.

"Here they are. I've taken them out of the packages and plugged them all in end to end, so now we'll have this really long strand of lights. I think this will be easier for you." She lifted the huge wad of lights above her head like it was the grand trophy for something.

Evie always meant well, but she just didn't think like regular people, people like us. A twenty-five-foot string of lights? Now that should be easy for Daddy to wind around this tree. Maybe if he had a couple of weeks and we moved the tree to the center of the room and put it on Mama's lazy Susan.

"I know you wanted hot chocolate tonight, and I'm so sorry. I forgot the milk when I got groceries today."

No. I wanted to stomp my foot. How could someone forget milk? "But we always have hot chocolate when we decorate the tree. Daddy, you have to go get milk." I thought maybe I needed to cut me some bangs to hide my red streak.

Evie piped in. "Oh, that's not necessary. I have it all figured out. I can make something like hot chocolate out of my protein powder. I think we have plenty of chocolate syrup, and we can heat our cups in the microwave. Or maybe we could heat some apple juice like it was apple cider if you don't want that."

Daddy looked at Evie, then at me, and back at Evie. "Either one of those sounds good. You decide."

Evie handed Daddy the wad of lights and returned to the kitchen. Chesler walked back into the living then and said, "I put my nickel in that jar. That jar's got a lotta nickels in it. What's Mom going to do with my nickels?"

"That's how many times you were caught running in the house, but you remembered and walked this time. I'm sure she'll do some good with that money that's teaching you the house is not for running. Probably she'll give it to some poor kids who don't have a house. You and Kate help me here." Daddy gave the end of the lights with the plug to Chesler and told him to back up. Chesler had backed all the way to the den before Daddy untangled that mess of lights.

By the time we finished wrapping that string of boring white lights around the tree, I was dizzy, and Evie was back with a tray of four Christmas mugs of something chocolate she had concocted and a plate of cookies. No warm milk cooked slowly on the stove to dissolve the chocolate Mama shaved and topped with marshmallows.

Evie gave Chesler his mug first. He asked, "What about the marshmallows? We always have marshmallows."

Evie made that sheepish face she made when she knew she'd forgotten something. "I'm sorry we didn't have milk or marshmallows. I made this with soy milk and my protein powder and a tiny bit of chocolate syrup. But we have cookies—ones with sprinkles. I thought you'd like these."

I looked into that Christmas mug. It looked like Evie had filled it with muddy creek water, and it smelled like Granny's house when she cooked collard greens. I wasn't about to be the first to taste it, so I waited. And store-bought cookies? I didn't know anybody ate store-bought Christmas cookies. The O'Donnells and the Hardings *made* Christmas cookies and candy.

Chesler took a big bite of the cookie covered in red sprinkles and washed it down with a big gulp of that chocolate mess. His eyes got big, and he looked at Daddy like he didn't know what to do. I thought he was going to spit it out like he used to spray his green peas when he was a baby, but he swallowed hard and long. Then he said, "Hmm, I never had this before. It's pretty good."

Evie's sheepish face disappeared when Chesler said that. She smiled like she had won at Uno. "And just think, you're going to be building big muscles drinking this protein shake."

I took a sip, ate a cookie, and waited a few minutes before I put my mug on the tray. "Come on, we gotta dress this tree up with all these ornaments. The lights are all done."

Evie glanced at the tree. "How do you know they're done? They're not on."

I answered before she did something to mess that up too. "Oh, that's the last thing we do. We put the angel on top and clean up around the tree. Then Daddy plugs in the lights."

Chesler held up both hands with his fingers crossed. "And we cross our fingers like this and hope the lights come on."

"Oh, I see. That's a good plan." Evie picked up the tray and went to the kitchen. Hers was the only empty mug.

We were putting on our special ornaments when Evie returned with a shopping bag filled with wrapped presents. She was about to put them under the tree, but I wasn't about to let that happen. Evie spent hours developing her own photos in her studio like a mad scientist, step by step, but she didn't know anything about decorating a Christmas tree. "Wait. We have to finish decorating and sweep up the needles from under the tree first. Then we'll put the Christmas tree skirt around the bottom. We don't put the gifts under the tree until all the decorating is done."

"Oh, I didn't know. I'm glad you have such a good memory about these things, Kate. I guess I was just too excited about these gifts. I love getting presents, and I especially love giving presents. What can I do to help?"

Daddy explained to her about our special ornaments that Mama had made and the ones we'd made for Mama. He handed her a box of gold balls, and she worked on those while we finished hanging our special ornaments. Then I pinched Chesler's ear and pointed to the chair. He got my message, jumped up, and got the bag I had hidden. He held the bag behind his back, walked over to Evie, and said,

"Look, Kate and me made you something special. We used to make Christmas thingies for Mama, and we didn't get to when she went to heaven. But now you're our mom, and we made these for you." Chesler started to open the bag.

I couldn't pinch his ear 'cause I was standing next to Daddy. But I couldn't let him do that. "Wait, Chesler. You're opening Evie's present. Let her open it."

He handed the bag to her. "I was just goin' to show it to you. I was helpin'."

Evie's face looked soft, and I thought she might cry. "You made these for me?"

Chesler nodded his head. "Uh-huh. We did. It's our tra . . . tra . . ." He turned to me. "Kate, what is that word? You know."

Evie answered before I could. "Tradition. It's your tradition. I don't know what to say except that I am so grateful, and it makes me happier than you know that I'm now a part of your tradition." She reached down and gave him a hug and looked over and smiled at me. "I think your mama would be so proud to know you're carrying on family traditions. She taught you some beautiful ones that you will have forever. And maybe we could make a new one or two as well."

She opened the bag. What was in there was my whole idea. Daddy and Aunt Susannah had helped me a little, but it was all my thinking. Daddy secretly got copies of the wedding pictures I wanted, and Aunt Susannah Hope gave me one of her fancy doilies that she stiffened, and I did the rest. I gave Chesler a picture of himself all dressed up in his suit and then one holding Evie's hand and looking up at her. He glued them back to back and framed them with popsicle sticks. There was glitter in places that it shouldn't have been, but Evie loved it anyway. For mine, I used the photo of the four of us standing on the stairs all dressed up and glued it to the fancy doily, trimmed it with red ribbon, and tied more ribbon at the top to hang it on the tree. The best part was I cross-stitched Christmas *1991* in red and sewed it to the doily. Mama had taught me to do that.

Evie made over my gift for her too. She hung her two ornaments on the tree next to each other. Daddy filled in all the spaces with red balls, green balls, silver ones, and all the ones with the redbirds on them. Then he said, "Okay, Kate, get the angel."

I went back to the stairs where the Christmas boxes were and took the angel out of the box. The Christmas after Mama died, Daddy had found a Christmas angel with red hair like Mama. She would still be with us, at the top of our tree.

Daddy was sweeping away the pine needles and Evie was putting the skirt around the Christmas tree when I got back. "Did you find the angel, Kate?"

"Yes, sir. She was in that fancy box to keep her safe."

"Well, then, Ches, climb up here on my shoulders. Let's put her up there and make sure she's straight. We don't want any fallen angels around here."

Chesler did just like Daddy said, and Daddy put him down. "Now can we plug in the lights? I want to do it." Before Daddy could say no, Chesler climbed around behind the tree and plugged them in. When he turned around to look, he let out one of his hollers. "What happened to the lights? They're all white."

Daddy came to the rescue again. "Evie really likes white lights, and ours were old and probably a tangled mess. She's the artist, and she thinks white lights would make the ornaments shine and stand out." Daddy backed away from the tree and went to Evie's side. "And you know, I think she's right."

Evie smiled at Daddy. "Oh, I'm so glad you think so.

It's a perfect tree, and I have plans for Sunday afternoon to finish the decorating. What do you say we make a trip to the woods out back and cut some pine and cedar and make us some real garlands to go on the stairs? It will be like going to the woods to cut down a tree. A real family outing and a new tradition."

Chesler was the first one to say anything, and he started his jumping up and down routine. "Yeah, we'll be like Indians out in the woods. I'll take my slingshot."

Daddy added, "Sounds like a plan. We'll get it done, and the house will smell like Christmas for sure. And maybe we should ask Luke and Lisa to join us."

I didn't tell Evie that's what we always did. She could just think it was all her idea. And I knew our lights weren't old and they weren't a tangled mess. I'd seen to it they were put up right last Christmas, but I kept my mouth shut. I missed the colored lights, but in a way, Evie was right about the ornaments standing out. Still, this just all felt weird. It was the first Christmas with Evie in the house.

I watched her put the presents under the tree. They looked like a professional had wrapped them in all that foil paper and fancy ribbons, not like our handmade wrapping. Store-bought cookies, creek-water hot chocolate, and fancy packages. This Christmas was gonna be different.

We watched a Christmas movie before bed. Before we said goodnight, Daddy reminded Chesler that he would be going to Aunt Susannah's tomorrow to play with Baby Hank and spend the night, and I'd be going out to Granny's. Daddy and Evie needed to go shopping. Or maybe they just needed some time away from Chesler and me.

I followed Chesler up the stairs. He climbed the stairs backward and stumbled into his room. That boy had a mind of his own, but Mama would be proud of him. She had always been full of fun and surprises—like Chesler. But me, I think I was born forty, and then when Mama died, I turned fifty. That didn't leave much time for fun and surprises.

If Granny took one look at me right now, she woulda said, "Girl, your red streak's a-shining, but I don't think you're mad. I think you have a classic case of the mully-grubs. You got to do something about that. Get busy if you want them to go away. Do something, girl." Granny Grace was right about most everything. I wanted the mullygrubs gone.

So I got busy and looked through my chest for my Christmas sweaters. I had two, but I didn't know if they'd fit this year. My arms were longer, but nothing else had changed much. I tried one on and put it in my bag to wear to church Sunday. Then I packed everything else I needed for my overnight at Granny's.

All that done, I got ready for bed and crawled under the sheets and wrote in my diary for a little while. Laramie was the only one that I ever let read my diary. It was mostly about Mama, and if Evie ever read it, she'd have the mullygrubs too. Granny said it would just take some time and getting used to having Evie around here.

My flannel nightgown felt so good. My quilt too. Mama had made it for me out of her clothes and some of my baby clothes. It covered my whole bed, and the redbird she'd embroidered in the middle was my favorite square. Mama's quilt and my redbird pictures were always around even if the real bird didn't show up.

Mama had known she was dying when she started making that quilt. But when her cancer got bad, she made Granny and Aunt Susannah Hope promise to finish it. It was my Christmas present from Mama that year after she went to heaven. She even wrote me a letter and left me a lock of her red hair in a silk bag.

I reached for that little bag under my pillow. I just couldn't stop thinking about Mama. Home seemed so strange these days, like it was somebody else's. Mama was gone, and now Evie was here. I liked her. I even loved her. But she wasn't Mama. She couldn't seem to get the grocery list right or the laundry or anything else around the house, and her cooking made Daddy's frozen fish sticks taste good. But she told Daddy and me she didn't want me helping out anymore. She said she wanted me to enjoy being a girl, and she would figure out how to run the house.

Evie was a world-renowned photojournalist, and I thought maybe she should stick to that. I liked it when she taught me about light and shadows and about telling my stories with my camera and the pictures I drew. I knew she was trying to fit into a house and family that used to be Mama's, and that she'd given up her career and travel until Daddy finished school next year. He'd always wanted to be a doctor, but he didn't get to be. He was the best paramedic in several counties, and now he was gonna be a real physician's assistant and work with Uncle Luke when he finished school.

I stared out my window at the stars twinkling through the bare limbs of the elm tree. Somehow the night sky made me think about heaven and Mama, and somehow I wasn't feeling so good about giving Evie her ornament. Maybe it was the right thing to do 'cause it put a smile on her face, but I hoped it didn't make Mama feel bad. I'd already had a talk with myself about this when I decided to do it. I knew I'd feel guilty if I didn't make an ornament for Evie, and now I felt guilty because I had.

I closed my eyes and whispered, "Mama, if you're listening, I love you. I'll always love you. I hope it's okay that I love Evie a little bit, and I hope my giving Evie her ornament didn't make you sad. Granny says there's no sadness in heaven. I hope she's right. I love you, Mama."

Chapter Two

———◆———

Kate

G ranny must have heard us driving up the lane because she was standing on the back porch steps when Daddy pulled into the driveway. Her red gingham apron flapped in that cold December morning wind, and she held her hands above her eyes to shield them from the bright sun reflecting off the snow.

Daddy honked the horn like he always did when he pulled into Granny's driveway. He put the truck in Park and let it idle to stay warm. "No guineas flying when I honked the horn. Too cold for them this morning. They must still be in the barn. Nearly too cold for me. We'll see you at church in the morning, and don't forget to tell Granny Grace I'm taking everyone to lunch tomorrow. So don't you let her start preparing lunch."

"I'll try, but you know Granny. She's got a mind of her own. Cooking makes her happy, and she likes it when we come to lunch."

"I know. But it's time we take her to lunch. You have a

fun day in the kitchen. I'm expecting some mighty fine Christmas goodies. And help Granny Grace keep the wood burning in the stove. I chopped her plenty of oak earlier this week. It's in the rack on the back porch."

"Yes, sir. You got Chesler's Christmas list?" That was my way of asking Daddy if he and Evie were going Christmas shopping or just needed some time off this weekend from Chesler and me. Having kids at Christmas or anytime was new to Evie. She'd only been an aunt before, and Daddy was trying to teach her about being a mom while he was still learning about being a daddy without Mama around.

Daddy winked at me. "Yes, ma'am. It's a good thing Christmas is a week and a half away. It may take me that long to find some of these things on Chesler's list."

"Yeah, I know. I helped him write his letter to Santa." I gave him my serious look. "Do you know his sizes?"

"Yes, ma'am, I do. Somewhere around a seven or an eight."

"What kid wants clothes for Christmas? Weird, but you know Chesler, and you know he likes jeans and cowboy shirts—plaid ones—and boots?"

"I believe I do."

I slid closer to Daddy and kissed his cheek. "You and Evie be careful."

"Yes, ma'am, and thank you again for being so sweet to her last night. She's trying, Kate. She doesn't want to take your mama's place, but it's hard for her to figure out what to do."

"I know, and you take her somewhere nice to lunch today. I mean really nice, and don't roll your eyes at me when I say that."

Daddy saluted me like I was some kind of drill sergeant. Maybe I sounded bossy like Granny Grace, but since Mama had gone to heaven, Daddy needed reminding about a lot of things. Mama had left lists for all of us, even Chesler, and she left a long list of things for me to remind Daddy to do.

I hopped out of the truck and trudged through the snow to the back door. Granny hugged me like it had been ten years since she and Evie took me shopping for a Christmas dress Wednesday. Mama and Granny always made my Christmas dresses, but Evie didn't know how to sew.

That had been some shopping trip. Not only did I get my first store-bought Christmas dress—a green velvet one—but Granny and Evie had decided it was time for me to get a bra. When they told me I should have a training bra, it made no sense to me. I mean, it wasn't like I was learning to ride a bicycle and needed training wheels, and I didn't even have anything to train. I guessed it was just training me to wear a bra whenever I really need one.

Granny finally let go of me, and I took a deep breath and said, "Good morning. You musta really needed a hug this morning."

"I always need a hug, and you did too. Everybody needs lots of hugs." Granny led the way and opened the kitchen door. I stepped inside and just stood there holding my bag for a minute. The winter-time smells of Granny's house slapped me in the face—oakwood burning in the potbellied stove in the corner, sweet spices, and strong coffee. "Something surely smells good."

"Oatmeal chewies. Second batch in the oven. Come on in, girl. It's cold, and we have things to do. I was up before the sun this morning getting things ready." Granny closed the door and used her foot to push a wadded-up towel back across the bottom of the door. "Every summer I tell myself I'm getting that fixed, and somehow I never do. But that old towel keeps the wind from coming under the door, and it's blowing cold this morning." She straightened her apron.

"Don't take your stuff to the bunk room. You'll be warmer in the guest room. Hurry up, now, and let's get started."

I walked around the counter. From the looks of the bags of flour and sugar and chocolate chips and butter, the baking aisle at the grocery store had to be empty 'cause it was all on Granny's counter. At least she didn't have to buy eggs. Her chickens gave Granny and her neighbors all the eggs they needed.

I walked through the kitchen and into the family room. There, in the corner where the Christmas tree usually stood, sat the curio cabinet holding all of Granny's pink Depression glass. Granny Grace musta been too busy to put up her tree. And there were no pine wreaths with red bows in the windows either. Not even a Christmas candle on the coffee table. Granny always had this farmhouse dressed for Christmas by now.

She and Grandpa had lived in an old Victorian house in town all their lives until they sold the store and retired. That was the house where Mama and Aunt Susannah grew up. Grandpa told me this farmland had belonged in the O'Donnell family for generations, and it was just sitting out here all by itself until they built this farmhouse for our family. Grandpa made sure every room had big windows to let the sunlight in all day long. The dining room was big enough for the wooden table he built out of logs cut from the property. He and Granny Grace had wanted a table big enough for the whole O'Donnell clan. They were hoping for lots of grandchildren to fill up this house, but that had changed when Mama went to heaven.

I passed the door to the bunk room Granny had designed for all the grandchildren. Grandpa built three solid bunk beds out of wood that was cut down when they cleared the land to build the house, and Granny covered every bed in a handmade quilt made by women in the family. Mama and Aunt Susannah Hope painted the walls sky blue, made curtains, and Mama even painted a mural of farm animals on one wall. So far, we each had an entire bunkbed to ourselves since it was just Chesler and me and Baby Hank. Granny had probably sent me to the guest room 'cause she thought I would be too sad in the big bunk room by myself. *Or maybe she thought I was too old for it since I'm wearing a bra now.*

I walked down the hall to her guest room and put my bag down. This room was filled with antiques, family heirlooms, lots of baskets, and curtains made of bandanas of every color. Grandpa had even built Granny a special set of shelves to go in front of the window 'cause her African violets liked morning light. This was a happy, comfortable room, not like Aunt Susannah Hope's house. She got the old Victorian when Granny moved out here, and everything there was either white or light pink and covered in lace. But Mama was like Granny. She'd liked cozy, comfortable, bright, and cheery, and I did too.

Granny was taking the cookies out of the oven when I got back to the kitchen. "Want one while they're hot?"

"Yes, ma'am. May I have a glass of milk? We were out of milk this morning. Evie forgot again. We had her protein powder with chocolate syrup last night for our hot chocolate. At least she did. I couldn't drink that mess. It wouldn't get past my nose."

I heard Granny's funny little giggle.

Granny handed me my favorite glass with the redbird on it. "Sure, there's a whole gallon in the fridge. Got to have milk if you're baking for Christmas."

I poured myself a glass of milk and sat down to the table with two warm, oatmeal chewy cookies in my hand. "Sometimes, I just wish Evie would let me make the grocery list like I used to. I always made the list like Mama said, and

I reminded Daddy when it was time to shop. But now Evie thinks she should be doing things like the grocery shopping, cooking, and laundry. And Granny, she's just awful at it. All of it."

I watched Granny Grace keep right on spooning cookie dough onto the cookie sheet. "Kate, how about cutting Evie a bit of slack? She and your daddy have only been married a couple of months, and she's never had a family before."

"I know. She's been traveling the world taking pictures and writing books, and she just doesn't think like normal people. She's different." I took a big gulp of milk.

Granny Grace never looked at me. "But you liked her because she was different. And look at all the things she's taught you about photography and light and color and telling stories with the pictures you take."

"I know. But maybe she should just keep doing those things and let me do the other stuff. I learned to do it pretty good. At least that's what Daddy says."

"Maybe Evie thinks it's time you started being a young girl again and not the woman of the house. You took on lots of responsibilities when your mama died, and Evie's there now to do those things."

I wiped the crumbs from my mouth. "Go back to being a little girl again? That's going to be kinda hard since I'm wearing a bralette."

Granny Grace stopped what she was doing and laughed out loud. "You're wearing a what?"

I started toward the sink with my empty milk glass. "A bralette. That's what Evie calls my training bra. She went back to the store and got two more Thursday while I was at school—a pink one and a beige one. She's real excited about these training bras."

"Well, that's a new one on me." She stopped laughing and started spooning out cookie dough again. "Sounds like she's a bit more excited than you are."

"It's okay. It's not like I really need one yet, and it's not like I don't know about wearing bras. Laramie's been wearing one for two years, and she never wore a bralette."

"Maybe Evie thinks this is some kind of rite of passage thing, and she's trying to make it a meaningful experience for you. Just go along with her, Kate. She's trying awfully hard to fit in. She knows she'll never take the place of your mama, and she's just trying to figure out this whole family thing and how to be what you need. It's easier with Chesler because he's so young, but it's not so easy with you since you've been the woman of the house."

"I know. It's just a lot to figure out. I love Evie, and I'm glad she married Daddy 'cause he's happy again. But it's just plain weird sometimes. She's nothing like Mama."

"She's more like your mama than you know, especially in her heart and in her goodness. And I believe she really loves you and Chesler. You know how that quilt your mama made you keeps you covered and warm and full of sweet memories? Well, Evie's trying hard to make a quilt of love, and it'll cover a lot of her shortcomings and make everything fine in the long run."

Granny picked up the tray of cookies. "Last batch. While they're baking, let's get started on my never-fail fudge, and then we'll make the peppermint bark to go on top. We don't have to worry about it setting up today. We only need to put it on the table on the back porch for five minutes."

I turned to the bookshelf at the end of the cabinet. "Where's the recipe? Which book?"

Granny didn't say a word. I turned to look at her to see if she heard me. She was standing there smiling, tapping her temple with her index finger. "Recipe's right up here, sweet girl."

"In your head? The recipe's not in one of these books?" I hesitated, "But what if . . .?"

"What if I die and the recipe is buried with me? Is that what you were about to say?"

"No, Granny. That's not what I was gonna say." Granny Grace always knew when I was telling a fib, but I told her one anyway. "I was gonna say what if I wanted to teach Evie how to make fudge. I need a copy of the recipe."

Granny Grace turned her head and looked doubtfully out of the corner of her eye. "Well, if that's the case, then maybe you should write it down as we make it."

I felt like Granny Grace needed another squeeze, so I hugged her. "Thanks. I never made fudge with Mama, so maybe this is something—a new tradition—I can start with Evie. I'm trying, too, Granny. I really am."

"Would you grab me two sticks of butter out of the fridge, please, and that can of evaporated milk on the counter? Still not calling her 'Mom,' are you?"

I opened the refrigerator and hesitated again. "Sometimes I do, but Chesler always does. He calls her 'Mom' all the time, and we had a talk about it. She likes him to call her 'Mom,' but she said it was okay if I wasn't ready."

"That's good. At least you're not calling her 'Miss Evie.' She's a wise and caring woman, and you're blessed to have her, Kate. I know we both miss your mama so much, especially around Christmas." Granny stopped peeling the paper off the stick of butter and turned to look at me. "I hate that we both lost your mama, but I'm so glad you and Chesler will grow up with Evie. I think Diana Joy would have liked her. Is the redbird still coming to your kitchen window?"

"Every day." I handed Granny another stick of butter. "Hey, I noticed you don't have your Christmas tree up yet. We could go cut one, and I can help you decorate today after we finish baking. That would be fun."

She turned around and reached for the bag of sugar on the counter. "Well, we need to have a little talk about that."

Before she could say more, her phone rang. On her way to answer it, she handed me back the other stick of butter. "Here, put the butter in the big pot on the stove, and add that can of milk and five cups of sugar. Stir it real good." I must have looked bug eyed 'cause Granny shook her head and said, "I'll make this short. You'll do just fine." She answered the phone and reached for her pad and pencil.

I watched the two sticks of butter melt and added the sugar while Granny listened to someone on the phone and wrote something on her notepad. She wasn't saying much. She turned to me and held her hand over the phone and asked, "Butter melted and you stirred in the sugar and milk?"

I nodded in agreement.

"When it comes to a boil, boil it for eight minutes exactly. Set the timer."

I nodded again and stared at the pot and heard Granny Grace say something about how going to the castle was something she'd always wanted to do and that she would get in her final deposit tomorrow at church. And something about her new Christmas sweater.

Granny Grace was planning something. She had no Christmas decorations up, and she was talking about a castle.

I kept watching the mixture. It was bubbling now, just like my insides. Where was Granny going and when?

"How long has it boiled?"

"Six minutes."

"Perfect. Keep stirring."

I kept stirring, watched the timer, and held my lips tight so I wouldn't say something. When the timer buzzed, I whispered loudly, "Granny, what do I do now?"

She said to her caller, "Hang on a minute, Henrietta. I need to help Kate with the fudge." She laid down the phone and grabbed a bag of chocolate chips on her way to rescue me. "Here, girl, pour these in and stir in this jar of marshmallow creme, and then stir like your life depended on it. I'll be done in just a minute to help you pour it in that pan over there by the sink. It'll take both of us."

I stirred until I thought that wooden spoon would break and there were no white streaks left of the marshmallow creme or chocolate chips. It was smooth chocolate. I kept stirring and listening. I could tell Granny was trying to be quiet, and she was still writing notes.

She finally hung up the phone, and she was right. It took both of us—her to hold the pot and me to spoon that fudge into the buttered pan.

Granny scraped the pot and smoothed the fudge with her spatula. "Okay, I'll put this on the porch, and while it cools, we'll make the peppermint bark to go on top. Would you open the door for me?"

"Yes, ma'am."

While Granny Grace was on the porch, I peeked at her notes—dates, eight-hundred-dollar balance to be paid Sunday, seven nights with semiformal dress on one night, returning Friday. Granny was going somewhere with somebody, and she hadn't told anybody.

When I heard Granny rattle the doorknob, I dropped her notepad on the desk like it was burning my hands and picked up the phone. When she got inside, I hung up the phone.

Granny Grace asked, "Somebody call?"

"No, ma'am, I was just trying to call Laramie." I knew my red streak had lit up my forehead 'cause I was upset and fibbing at the same time.

The Christmas Portrait Surprise

Granny Grace put another piece of wood in the stove and washed her hands. "I thought you said Laramie was going shopping with her mother."

"She is. I was just calling to see if she left yet."

I wanted to know about Granny's trip a whole lot more than Chesler wanted a new pair of boots for Christmas. But how was I going to find out without her knowing that I was snooping? She would not like that. All my thoughts and ideas were churning like the cookie batter in Granny's mixer, but I let them settle in my rattled head a minute, and I figured it out. I couldn't just ask her, but I could ask her again. "I didn't see your Christmas tree or your wreaths on the windows. Want to decorate this afternoon after we finish the baking?"

Granny Grace just turned around from the sink and looked at me.

Chapter Three

———— ◆ ————

Sunday, December 15
Cedar Falls

Kate

I fidgeted through church. I wanted to sit with Laramie and her mom, but Granny Grace wanted us to sit together as a family. With the four of us and Granny and Aunt Susannah Hope and Uncle Don and Uncle Luke and Aunt Lisa, we filled up a pew—the second one on the organ side. Little Hank was in the nursery.

Pastor Simmons—that was Evie's brother—was preaching up a storm about what it must have been like to be Joseph and Mary at the very first Christmas. He knew how to tell that story and make it come alive, talking about how young they were and leaving their homes and traveling to a place on foot with Mary about to give birth. And then they couldn't find a room.

I couldn't think about Mary and Joseph on a trip for Christmas 'cause all I could think about was what Granny Grace was going to tell us at lunch today. She'd told me yesterday she would explain it all today and that was that. Things had stayed quiet for the rest of the day yesterday. I knew she was going somewhere, but I didn't know where or how far, and I couldn't tell her how I knew. I hoped she couldn't find a room in the inn, either, and she would have to come home.

I was never so glad for a sermon to be over and to hear that last stanza of "Go, Tell It on the Mountain." We stood to sing, and Daddy picked Chesler up and let him stand on the pew. Daddy held him close so he wouldn't fall. Chesler had caused more than one disaster in church in his short life. He knew the chorus, and he was singing louder than anyone, even louder than the tenors in the choir. I could feel everybody's eyes on the Hardings. What I didn't know was if they were thinking *that boy surely can sing,* 'cause he really could, or if they were wondering why Daddy would let him stand on the pew and sing so loud. I didn't care. I just wanted outta there.

Since we hadn't gone to the Blue Cow on Friday night, we all went to lunch there today. It had been Mama's favorite place, but we didn't come to the Blue Cow for a long time after she went to heaven. After a while, though, Granny got us to start going again. It was still our favorite family place. Evie didn't really like the Blue Cow so much. Kale and broccoli were not on the menu, and she was not about to eat a burger or anything else that had passed through a frying pan. She was good about going there, though, 'cause she knew we liked it.

The only waitress we ever had at the Blue Cow was Miss Myrtle. She looked older than Granny with her purple hair and pruney skin and shiny blue eye shadow. I think she had smoked too many cigarettes 'cause when she talked, she growled. "Well, a happy Lord's Day to you folks. Missed you Friday night." All she had to do was ask one question. "So does this clan want your usual Friday-night supper for Sunday lunch?"

Daddy was sitting at the head of the table. He raised his eyebrows like that was his way of asking. Everybody nodded, and the waitress scribbled something on her pad and said, "It'll be out shortly."

Miss Myrtle was halfway to the kitchen when Granny said, "Wait a minute, Myrtle. Skip the fried fish for me. I'll have a salad just like Evie."

The waitress came back to our table and looked at Granny like she might have ordered a roasted rat. "Grace O'Donnell, that's a first. In all these years, I ain't ever brought anything to this table for you 'cept fresh fried perch, fries, coleslaw, and hushpuppies with sweet tea. Maybe there was a time or two you got the cheese grits, but a salad?" She used her eraser and scribbled something else. "Got it. All I can say is it's a mighty cold day for salad."

Granny answered, "Thank you, Myrtle. I'm sure I'll enjoy that salad, cold or not. Just consider it my new adventure."

A new adventure? I was itching to just stand up and ask, "So, Granny, is that the only adventure you're about to take?" I knew she was going somewhere, but she wouldn't say. Granny Grace had no business leaving us for Christmas, and she deserved to be put on the hot seat. She was the one who was always saying loving families weren't supposed to have secrets. She kept telling me that when Daddy was dating Evie. I was confused and trying to get used to the idea, and Granny Grace told me to try to accept Evie and be honest with Daddy about how I felt and not to keep secrets.

I looked at the clock on the wall above the cash register. It was made out of an old boat paddle and looked like something Grandpa might have made. It was twelve forty. I was giving Granny Grace until twelve forty-five to make her announcement, or I was asking the question. I would make her tell us. She didn't have to tell me yesterday, but Aunt

The Christmas Portrait Surprise

Susannah Hope would get Granny to tell even if she had to start hyperventilating like she did when Chesler picked up one of her porcelain ladies with an umbrella.

Twelve forty-four, and my heart was beating so fast I thought I might hyperventilate. I knew my red streak was redder than usual. I could feel it. I was about to open my mouth when Granny Grace announced, "Well, I have something I want to tell you all. Susannah knows, and she knows how I am excited about this. I'll be taking a trip."

Uncle Luke was sitting at the corner of the table right across from Evie. He looked and sounded just like Daddy. "Granny Grace, now that's just like you. Here it is December, and you're already planning your summer's vacation. I like the way you think ahead. Guess you have to make plans to get somebody to cover running Cedar Falls while you're gone."

Granny Grace grinned. "Cedar Falls will be fine without me, and at my age, Luke, you don't plan a trip that far ahead. This is something I've always wanted to do, and now I have the opportunity. I'm leaving Friday, and I'll be gone a week."

I knew it. She was leaving us for Christmas. I had a million questions, but I felt like I wasn't really there, like I was watching a movie and nobody could hear me if I spoke.

Aunt Susannah Hope was all bubbly. "She's going to Highlands, North Carolina, to spend a couple of days at a historic inn and then back for Christmas at the Kentucky Castle near Lexington. Oh, I wish I could go with her. To see those sights at Christmas! They'll really be something. She promised to take lots of pictures."

They could just all go with her, and I'd spend Christmas by myself. First Grandpa had gone to heaven, then Mama, and now Granny Grace was going to North Carolina. Three empty chairs at the Christmas table—only there wouldn't even be a Christmas table. I just wanted to go home and sit at my window and wait for the redbird. At least the bird showed up just like Mama said.

Evie asked, "Is this the group Matt is driving to Asheville?"

"Yes, it is. That brother of yours is one fine pastor to drive the six of us XYZs to North Carolina Friday. And then Roger Minton will be our driver back to Lexington for Christmas at the castle and then home the following Friday."

I still couldn't speak, but Chesler asked, "Granny, what's XYZs?"

Everybody at the table laughed but me. I was just a whole heap o' mad at Granny. That castle would still be there after Christmas, and she could take Aunt Susannah Hope and her old friends then, but she had no business leaving us at Christmas.

Granny chuckled. "Chesler, XYZ stands for 'extra years of zest.' Some folks would say 'maturing adults,' but we're really just old folks. I suppose XYZs is a nicer way of saying it."

Chesler poked his nose in it again. "Is that kind of like calling the bathroom the powder room?"

Everybody laughed at him, but I didn't. There was nothing to laugh about.

Granny Grace answered, "I suppose it is, Chesler. Anyway, it's just two old men and four old ladies like me who want to do something different for Christmas. One of them has no family, and the others have family that lives off somewhere and who won't be coming home for the holidays. They decided to take a trip together for Christmas, and I thought it was time I joined them."

Daddy looked at me like he was waiting for me to say something, but if Granny Grace didn't have to talk to me yesterday, I didn't have to say anything right now. Daddy said, "Grace, I don't know what to say." He paused. "We will miss you, but if this is something you truly want to do, then I say do it."

Granny Grace nodded at Daddy like she was glad he approved. "That's exactly what I was thinking. I'll miss all of you, too, but we can have another Christmas when I get back." She looked down at her hands in her lap and laced her fingers together. She looked a little bit sad. "I don't know how many more Christmases I have on this planet, but it looks like I'll have this one." Then she raised her head, and I think she put on a pretend smile. "Anyway, I need something different this Christmas. I've been thinking about this since Henrietta made the announcement, and I just decided to go. I'll be back before you have time to miss me."

Then everybody started talking around the table, laughing and asking Granny all kinds of questions like they were excited about her going. They were like background noise to what was going on in my head, but I wasn't really listening 'cause I didn't want to hear it. I didn't want to know it. I didn't want them to be happy about Granny Grace going away. I wasn't.

Miss Myrtle delivered our food—nine plates on two large trays and a bowl of pudding for Baby Hank. I watched her balance the trays on the palms of her hands, holding them on her shoulders, secretly wishing she'd just drop them all so we could go home. But I knew she'd never dropped a tray in her whole life, and if she did, I'd have to sit there even longer until they cooked it all again. This was worse than the mullygrubs. Much worse.

Everybody was still talking and laughing while I stared at two fried perch filets on my plate. Usually, I would have scarfed them down with a French fry in between every bite. But when I tried, that fish got bigger and bigger in my mouth until I couldn't swallow. I wasn't about to be excused, 'cause then they'd all make a fuss over me when I was just wanting to disappear.

Granny looked over at my plate. "Sweet girl, you're not eating much today. You have not touched that piece of perch or your hushpuppies."

I stared at my plate and didn't even look up. "I'm not hungry."

"Well, let's don't let that fish go to waste. Too many hungry people in the world."

I speared the untouched filet with my fork and dumped it on top of what was left of her salad. I didn't say a word, and I didn't look at Granny. But I knew she was looking at me with that look on her face that said, "Girl, you know better."

Granny Grace was right. I did know better. But I wasn't planning on doing better today. If she had the right to leave at Christmas, then I had the right to be mad about it.

When we finished eating, I was the first one out the door and went straight for the back seat of our car. Since Evie had joined our family, there was no more fussing over who got the front seat. It was always Evie.

I watched Daddy follow Granny Grace to her truck. They huddled while Evie pinched Baby Hank's cheeks. I imagined Granny and Daddy were talking about me and my behavior, but I didn't care.

Daddy brought my overnight bag and opened the backseat door and put it in my lap. I didn't turn my head, just my eyes to see if I could see Granny. I thought she was waving goodbye, but I just held on tight to my overnight bag.

All the way home, Evie talked about our afternoon adventure in the woods to cut holly and pine branches to make the garlands. Daddy went along with her like we'd never done that before, and Chesler was excited that Uncle Luke and Aunt Lisa were coming over to go with us. I didn't say a word. I had to figure something out. I was not going on that happy hunting party.

I was the first one through the door and up the stairs the second we got home. From the looks of Granny and Daddy's huddling, I figured he'd be banging on my door by the time I changed clothes.

I figured wrong. I didn't even have my Christmas sweater off before Evie was tapping. "Kate, are you all right?"

No, I was not. Nothing was right anymore, but I had to come up with something in a hurry. "I'm not feeling so good."

"May I come in?"

Mama woulda never asked for permission. She woulda been barreling through that door by now, but not Evie.

"Sure, you can come in."

Evie walked over to me and lifted my chin. "So you're not feeling well? I noticed you didn't eat much of your lunch."

"I didn't feel like eating."

"Is it your stomach?"

"I think so. I just want to lie down and take a nap. Maybe I'll feel better then." I finished taking off my sweater.

Evie felt my forehead. "No fever. Your head is cool."

"Good. Maybe that's a sign I'll feel better soon, but I don't think I feel like going out in the woods to cut the greenery."

Evie took my hands and led me over to sit on the side of my bed. "Kate, it's fine if you don't want to go, but you must tell me the truth. Are you really sick, or are you just sad that Granny Grace won't be here for Christmas? If you're feeling sick, Uncle Luke can come up and take a look at you when he gets here. But . . . your face is telling me a different story."

Caught, and I knew my red streak was showing. Evie was an expert at faces. She studied them for her photographs. I held tight to my tears, but my bag of sadness and madness was about to burst, and I really didn't want it to get all over Evie. I truly didn't. "I'm a little sad, and I don't feel good. I just want to be by myself."

I felt Evie's arm go around my shoulder. "Kate, we're all disappointed Granny Grace will be gone, and I imagine you're more disappointed than anyone, and I am so sorry. I know Christmas without your mama makes you sad, but it makes your granny sad too. She misses your mama and your granddad. So, for a change, we must think about what would make Granny Grace happy. Don't you think she deserves a little happiness?"

I was sniffling by then. "But going away won't make Granny happy. I know it won't. And what if it's her last Christmas? She likes being with her family, and she'll just be packing up her sadness and carrying it with her and making all of us sad at the same time."

"That could be true, Kate, but it's still Granny's choice."

"But why would Granny Grace choose to make all of us so sad by leaving? I don't care about how beautiful some old castle is. Making all of us sad won't make her happy."

Evie stood up and faced me. "Maybe not. But it's still her choice. Would you like me to go and have a talk with her? I could go tomorrow."

I sobbed. "If you think that would work, then you don't know nothing about Granny Grace. She does not have ears to hear when her mind is made up. She won't listen. She's going. You'd just be wasting your time."

"Well, then, would you like me to stay a while with you? We could postpone our outing to the woods."

Daddy walked in about that time. "What's going on in here?"

The Christmas Portrait Surprise

Before I could say a word, Evie answered. "Kate's not feeling so well."

Daddy came over and felt my head like Evie had. "No fever. Is it your stomach? You coming down with a cold? Sore throat, maybe?" Then Daddy looked straight at me. "But I see tears—big ones—and red eyes."

Evie answered for me again. "John, you don't have to be sick not to feel well. Kate is upset because Granny's leaving for Christmas. She has a right to be sad. We will all miss Granny Grace."

Daddy patted me on the head. "If that's all, then get your clothes changed, and let's go get happy. Uncle Luke just called, and they're on their way, and we'll be making tracks through those woods this afternoon cutting pine limbs and gathering pinecones and holly. You might even see a redbird or two."

"I really don't feel like going, Daddy. Could I just stay in my room and take a nap?"

"So you're going to pull a Granny Grace on us? We're all together having fun, and you're up here in your room feeling sorry for yourself?"

"That's not what she's doing. Granny's not feeling sorry for herself or us. She's just going off with her friends to have fun."

Daddy's worry lines showed beneath his wool cap. "Kate, listen to yourself . . ."

I knew he was about to light into me, but Evie interrupted him. "John, as good as you are, you don't understand females sometimes. But you're not the only man in the world who doesn't. Let's give Kate some space. She's a smart girl, and she knows how she feels and what she needs." Evie looked over at me and winked. "Maybe she'll feel better by the time we get back, and maybe she'll help us with some real hot chocolate. I made sure we had milk and marshmallows for our afternoon, and I'm certain Kate knows how to make it."

Daddy looked at me. "Kate, is that what you want? Just to be left alone?"

"Yes, sir, it is." I really didn't want Daddy to worry or ruin their good time. "Besides, I'm working on a project." I was fibbing. I did have a project to work on—Granny's Christmas present—but I wasn't about to work on that today.

"Okay, but we'll miss you. Who's going to tell me not to cut the holly close to the house so the redbird will stay near?" Daddy took Evie's hand and walked out my door.

"Thanks." I said softly. "Wait to cut the holly until you're deep in the woods."

I lay on my bed and curled up under the quilt Mama had made for me. It wasn't long before I heard Chesler hollering. That boy did everything, and I mean everything, big and loud, and he was probably wrapped around Uncle Luke's knees right now.

When the door slammed and things got quiet, I jumped up and looked out the window. They were headed down to the creek. Probably they would follow the creek into the woods. Daddy and Uncle Luke were out front with their hatchets, and Evie and Aunt Lisa followed them with large buckets. Chesler was just running rings around them as they walked through the snow.

We lived in town, but our house was at the end of the street and bordered the forest. Nelson's Creek ran along the back side of our property, and the woods were our neighbors. When the weather was warm, getting to fish in the stream at the end of the day made Daddy happy. And there was always wildlife, especially the birds.

When Daddy had talked to me about asking Evie to marry him, he'd said he would have to talk to her about where she wanted to live. I had never lived anywhere else, and leaving this house would have been like leaving every bit of Mama behind. I loved Evie more when she told Daddy she would be happy right here. At least where we lived didn't change when everything else did.

I stood at the window and waited for the redbird to perch in the elm tree. Before Mama died, she'd asked me to choose something that would always remind me that she loved me. I chose the redbird because Mama could sing more beautiful than any bird, and her hair was red. I waited for a little while, but no redbird.

I lay back down and thought about Christmas, remembering how it was with Mama. She had made everything special, and Granny Grace and Aunt Susannah Hope tried to keep that going. But with Granny away, everything would change. No real family Christmas. No Christmas Eve supper of Granny's French onion soup and grilled cheese sandwiches. No going to church for the Christmas Eve service and then going back to Granny's for the bonfire and skating in the moonlight. No Christmas-morning cinnamon buns at our house. No Christmas tablecloth to sign on Granny's long dining table 'cause there'd be no Christmas dinner.

Without Granny Grace, there'd be no Christmas for me. She had to stay. That meant I had to come up with a plan to make her stay. I was thinking hard about that when I heard a chirp. I rolled over and looked out the window. There she was, the cardinal, sitting on the bare limb of the elm tree in the afternoon sunlight.

"You always show up when I need you, little bird. I need your help, 'cause I need a plan. A good one."

Chapter Four

———— ◆ ————

Monday morning, December 16
Cedar Falls

Granny Grace

*A*nother cold and blustery morning made it a perfect day to make divinity. Susannah Hope thought she needed my help to make it, and I must say, coming to her rescue eased my conscience a bit about leaving for Christmas. I dressed for the cold, cranked up the truck, and went to the coop to gather the eggs while the truck was warming. That truck took longer to warm up these days than it took for milk to go sour, so I dreaded that ten-minute drive to town. At least the roads were clear.

I made it to Susannah Hope's home without incident. After I'd flattened ten feet of her boxwood hedge trying to back out of her driveway a few months back, I began parking on the street out front. Now I just needed to get up the hill to her front porch without breaking my eggs or one of my fragile old bones.

Susannah Hope met me at the front door. "Oh, you brought eggs? I didn't know if you would have any, so I bought three dozen Saturday."

I handed her the basket and walked in, shedding my coat, scarf, and gloves. "Well, if I didn't have Rhode Island Reds, I wouldn't. But I keep the coop warm, and they just keep laying all winter." I hung my coat on the rack behind the front door. "Besides, you know these egg whites are better than store-bought ones. We want divinity that will set up solid and is fluffy in the middle. I don't want anybody breaking a tooth with my confection. And it's the perfect day—cold and no humidity." I followed Susannah Hope into her kitchen. "Evie here yet?"

"Not yet, but she should be here any minute. Said she had to go by Ponder's Print Shop and pick up the Christmas cards Luke had printed. It's just like Luke to send Christmas cards to all his patients, and I think Lisa designed them. The print shop wasn't open early enough for Lisa to pick them up and deliver them to Luke's office before school." Susannah Hope put the egg basket on the kitchen island. "How about a cup of coffee or tea? We need to give these eggs a few minutes to get to room temperature before we start beating the whites."

"Coffee sounds good." I walked over to Baby Hank's table where he was putting a wooden puzzle together. "Good morning, Hank. Looks like you already started having fun without me."

"Hey, Gwanny." He held the puzzle piece in his hand up high enough for me to see. "I don't know where the gween piece goes."

"Look in the corner where the *wedbird* is perched. Maybe it goes up there in the tree."

I didn't miss the look Susannah Hope gave me when I mocked Baby Hank's speech.

I sat down at the breakfast table to catch my breath. "Shouldn't take long to warm the eggs in this hot house you live in, and I tried to keep them warm on the floorboard of the truck." I reached in the pocket of my denim barn jacket for a tissue to wipe the sweat on my brow. Walking up the hill did that to me lately. "I think I'll take a small glass of water to go with my coffee."

Susannah Hope poured me a cup, and just as she brought it to me, the doorbell rang. She went to the front door and brought Evie to the kitchen. As if on cue, Baby Hank jumped up from his table, grabbed his pants, and screamed like they were on fire. "Bafwoom!"

Susannah Hope sprinted through the kitchen, picked him up, and ran down the hall.

Evie looked puzzled and headed for the coffee pot. "Is Hank okay?"

"For sure, he's okay. Don't know about Susannah, though. I figure it's probably lesson number one hundred eighty-three in Baby Hank's ongoing potty training. That boy's a little manipulator. Susannah Hope read all the books and decided it wasn't wise to rush him, but I told her it was time to start when he's bringing her a dry diaper because he's wet his. So lately, his new trick is screaming, and Susannah Hope comes running and takes him to the potty."

Evie giggled and came to the table with her steaming cup of java. "I hope they made it." Her happy face didn't last long. "I missed all of that fun with Kate and Chesler. I can thank Diana Joy for handling that part and for bringing up two wonderful kids."

"Yes, she did a fine job. She was a good mother and loved them more than life." I felt the melancholy wash over me just thinking about how things used to be. "And Evie, I believe that Diana Joy would be happy to know you're picking up and carrying on with them now, and that you and John are building a life together."

Evie's eyes were piercing as she looked straight at me. "Grace, you are the most remarkable woman I know. I have taken pictures of women all over the world—mothers who were starving themselves so there would be enough food to feed their own children and mothers who walked for miles every day to get clean water for their families. I've seen firsthand that God knew what He was doing when He created mothers. And it's a natural thing for them to take care of their children. But to have lost your daughter and welcomed another woman into your family with your grandchildren? That is beyond the call of mother duty."

"I don't think it has anything to do with mother duty. Oh, I miss my daughter, but I love my grandchildren, and I believe you do too. You're good for them and for John. How could I not be pleased about that?" I gripped my coffee mug to warm my cold fingers.

"I'm grateful you're pleased, Grace, but still, it must be tough. I remember when John and I first realized that our love was real and we weren't sure what to do about it. I had no one else to talk to about my feelings and my fears, but you listened to me and told me the truth. You talked straight to me about your feelings and how the road ahead with the children, especially Kate, could get bumpy." Evie got quiet and gazed out the bay window a moment before she turned back to me. "Well, the road's bumpy, Grace. Really bumpy right now."

I knew what that bump was, and I knew what had caused it. I had not missed Kate's silence Saturday afternoon and yesterday. "So, tell me what's going on with my sweet girl."

Evie expressed no surprise that I knew and answered, "She's just so sad. Kate can be such a bright, creative, thoughtful, and fun young girl, but sometimes there is this sadness, such a raw and deep sadness, that comes over her." Evie paused. "I just don't know . . . I don't know how to fix it. I hate seeing her this way."

"I've seen it. She's mad and sad. Holidays have been hard for her since Diana Joy died. I told you how her mother made such a big to-do over holidays and birthdays, and now when those events come around, they bring with them memories that warm Kate's heart one minute and send her to a dark place the next. And as I said, she's mad. She's angry with me right now because I'm taking my trip."

Evie stared into her coffee cup. "I don't want to dump her sadness on you and put a damper on your plans, but you're right."

"Did she talk to you about it?"

"Actually, she did. When we got home yesterday, she went straight to her room. John thought she was ill, but I sensed it was something else. So I went up to check on her. We had somewhat of a conversation, but I felt she needed some time and space. John pushed her to go with us to cut the greenery, but I persuaded him not to push so hard and to let her own her feelings. She stayed in her room all afternoon and evening. I took her some soup and a sandwich and checked on her again before bedtime, but she was still quiet and sad."

"How was she this morning?"

"I think she was a bit better. I thought maybe she would try to get out of going to school today, but she didn't. She was up, dressed, and downstairs right on time and frustrated with me because I couldn't find my keys again. She was still quiet, though. When I dropped her off at school, she wanted to know if she could invite Laramie for a sleepover on Wednesday night. Of course, I said yes. A girl needs her best friend. I'm hoping that will bring her around."

"Kate's angry with me. When she was with me Saturday, she suspected something when Henrietta called, but I just wasn't ready to tell her about my plans. She started stewing about it then, and when she asked me and I didn't tell, that probably made things worse. I think I chickened out and sensed a need for reinforcements, so that's why I waited until Sunday when we were all together to make my announcement."

Evie nodded like the picture was clearing up. "While we were talking, I asked her if she'd like for me to talk to you and see if I could persuade you to stay."

"What did she say to that?"

"Shook her head like she meant business. Said it was no use since your mind was made up and you didn't have ears to hear. Is that true, Grace? I mean, I want you to be happy if this trip would make you happy, but would you have ears to hear me?"

I hesitated before I spoke. "Kate's right. My mind is made up, and my bags are half packed. It's not like we won't have a family Christmas gathering. We just won't have it on Christmas Day. And seeing the Kentucky Castle and the Old Edwards Inn at Christmas? Well, that's something I've always wanted to do, and this year the time's right." That was all I could tell her. It was the truth, just not all of the truth. I wasn't sure if I was ready to tell Evie my real reason for leaving or even if she was ready to hear it.

"Then I won't try to talk you out of it. We'll just plan something that will make Kate happy until you get back." She paused again before seriously asking, "But one more thing. Grace, is there something you're not telling us? Kate's worried that it could be your last Christmas, and that you're just trying to prepare us."

Well, that one put me on my feet. I walked around the table to Evie, hoping she had ears to hear. "Only the good Lord knows if this is my last Christmas, and He's not given me any reason to think that it is. But Evie, you all are a family now, and it's time you make some of your own traditions, and I don't think you'll do that with ol' Granny

Grace around here barking orders and making all the plans, trying to hang on to some things that need changing."

Evie looked up at me, her frown telling me she still had questions. "You're doing this for me? You think I should be making new Christmas traditions for this family? I can tell you right now, if that's your reason, it's not a good one. Grace, I've never had a family for Christmas, only my brother's. And you O'Donnells and Hardings have some beautiful traditions that fill a void for me. What do I know about creating Christmas traditions? Until I met John and Kate and Chesler, I never knew what continent I would be on for Christmas. And now I have the gift of a family with built-in beautiful traditions that don't need changing. Please don't make this trip on my account."

Before I could respond, Evie continued. "And besides, you're so much more than just Granny Grace. John was young when he lost his parents, and he thinks of you as his mother. You know that. He loves you and depends on you. We both do, and whether you know it or not, that makes you a mother-in-law of sorts to me. And you're the only grandmother Kate and Chesler have. What kind of person would I be not to appreciate and respect these relationships?"

I could see that Evie was close to tears. I reached out and wrapped my arms around her. "You're the kind of person who says the things I need to hear. You know I've never lied to you about my feelings, and I'm not about to start now. I loved Diana Joy more than I have words to say, and I miss her that much too. But I have grown to love you like a daughter since you came into our lives. This family's had so much loss, and you're the best thing that has happened to all of us in quite a while."

She stood and hugged me. With her chin still on my shoulder, she asked, "Does this mean you'll stay?"

I pulled away and held her hands. "No. It means I love you. I love all of you, but I'm doing this. And when I get home from my trip, we'll have our Christmas. A different kind of Christmas, but it'll still be ours."

Susannah Hope returned to the kitchen with fresh clothes on Baby Hank. "Well, he didn't make it to the bathroom, so we had a clean-up job. I tell myself I must be patient. He will learn in his own time."

I wanted to pat Susannah Hope on the head, but I patted Hank instead and agreed. "So, let's get busy. It's a perfect day for making divinity."

Evie took her last sip of coffee. "Then I'll leave you two to it. I need to deliver these cards to the office for Luke, and then I have some work in my darkroom. And don't ask. Remember, it's Christmas, and this family is into home-made personal gifts."

Susannah Hope was puzzled. "But I thought you were coming to spend the morning."

"Wish I could, but I can't. I just needed to talk to Grace. She always knows what to say and what to do." Evie started to walk away but turned. "And she did. That saying and doing part."

I was weary of the weightiness of this conversation and lightened the mood when I snapped my fingers and spun around on my toes. "Glad I got somebody fooled. I got plenty to say about plenty of things, but for now, let's get that mixer going. And do you already have the pecans chopped?"

Evie left, and we started to work. Alone most of the time at the farm, I was accustomed to peace and quiet, just the dog barking once in a while and the guineas squawking. So much heavy conversation and constant racket were wearing on me, especially when my head was so noisy with worry about Kate. I didn't want to be the cause of any more pain for that child, but I knew what I was doing was the best for all of us.

No more quiet puzzles for Baby Hank. He was banging the kitchen-cabinet doors, opening and slamming them shut one at a time and then starting all over. "I understand why you look tired all the time, Susannah Hope. I had forgotten that toddlers are noisy and how busy little people are constantly moving and exploring. And just think, the older they get the busier they are, and the noise they make is of a different kind."

———•———

Monday early afternoon

Kate

Only three days of school this week and then Christmas break. Evie had said I could invite Laramie for a sleepover Wednesday night, but we were almost late to school again this morning, and I didn't have a chance to ask her.

Laramie was my best friend, and she was so smart—more like street smart, Daddy said. Three years ago, she wasn't the kind of girl I would've invited for a sleepover. She was always in trouble at school, she made bad grades, and the words that came out of her mouth woulda caused Granny to use a whole bar of soap. Laramie's family had its share of troubles with her mom's drinking and her dad's anger problems. Her mom finally just up and left Laramie and her dad one day and went to her sister's to get some help for herself, but Laramie didn't know where she was or even if she was dead or alive. As bad as it was for me, at least I knew Mama was in heaven.

We had both been girls without their mamas. Laramie

was the one person in my class who understood when Mama died. She was the only one who would talk to me about her. But that Christmas, my first one without Mama, Laramie's dad hurt her and she ran away. That changed everything.

The police and Daddy searched for her all night and the next day, and Granny Grace and I prayed that God would stop the snow until Laramie was found. The next night, Laramie showed up at our house because she had nowhere else to go. Daddy took her to the hospital, and two days later, we brought her home to be with us for Christmas. Her mama was gone and her daddy went to jail for some things I didn't know about. Daddy got busy tracking her mama down, and her mama showed up on Christmas Eve, knocking on our door to take Laramie home. It was Laramie's best Christmas ever. I was glad for her even though I knew my mama wasn't going to be walking through our front door for Christmas.

Granny Grace told me when folks like Laramie's parents didn't like themselves and didn't understand how much God loved them, then they didn't know how to love each other no matter how hard they tried. That was why they did bad things. Granny Grace said it was our job to love them and teach them how to love each other, and they would start doing good things. So, when Mr. Fields got out of jail, Daddy helped him to go to counseling and started having lunch with him once a week, and Granny Grace got Mrs. Fields to be a part of her church ladies' group that took care of poor people. With all that going on, the right kind of loving started growing at the Fields' house, and that made Laramie so happy.

Laramie became my best friend, sorta like the sister I'd always wanted. She didn't say dirty words anymore except once in a while when one just slipped out, and she was one of the smartest students in our class. No more getting into trouble.

The lunch bell wasn't finished ringing before I made a beeline for Laramie, and we walked together to the cafeteria. "Hey, Evie told me you called last night. I'm sorry I didn't know. She didn't tell me until this morning."

Laramie picked up a tray. "It's okay. I was surprised to see you at school today. I thought maybe you were sick, and then you were so late."

"No, I'm fine, but Evie couldn't find her keys again. Her head's always somewhere taking pictures, and she can't remember to put her keys where they belong." We filled our lunch trays and found a place to sit where there was nobody else around.

"You don't sound fine. You sound grumpy to me." Before she took a bite of anything, she opened her carton of milk and gulped it. "You drinking yours?"

I handed her my milk. "No, you can have it." I stared at my plate and picked up the roll sitting there. "How am I supposed to spread this cold butter on a cold roll?"

Laramie elbowed me as she took a bite of macaroni and cheese. "Yeah. Like I said, you sound grumpy."

"Hey, you want to sleep over Wednesday night? I already asked Evie, and she said yes."

"Will you still be grumpy, or do you think you'll be over it by then?"

I thought about it. "Maybe. I'm not sure, but I need your help. And besides, you're not always Miss Sunshine yourself."

Laramie kept eating. "True. Don't tell me you haven't finished your Christmas presents. Oh, but it's okay. I'll help you."

"It's not that. You remember when your mom left and you ran away and she came back home?"

She turned toward me with her eyes blaring. "Kate, you really think I'd forget something like that? I don't think so.

But what are you bringing it up for now?"

"Granny Grace is going away for Christmas with a bunch of her friends. She's going to some old castle and an inn in North Carolina. And without her, we won't be having Christmas. You have to help me think of something I can do so that she has to stay here. Or you have to help me with what I'm thinking."

"Katherine Joy Harding. I already know what you're thinking, and you need to forget it. This smells like trouble to me. Trouble for everybody."

"Not if it keeps Granny Grace at home for Christmas."

Chapter Five

———— ♦ ————

Tuesday morning, December 17
Cedar Falls

Granny Grace

I grabbed my jacket and headed for the door, knowing I'd better crank up my truck so that I wouldn't be a wrinkled-up popsicle in a red quilted barn jacket when I got to the church. I knew I needed to get rid of this old truck, but it was used to me, and I was used to it. What did I need with one of those new-fangled trucks with electric seats, a four-speed automatic transmission, power windows, and dual fuel tanks—the kind John drove? I had a hard enough time keeping one tank filled, and what on earth would I do without my stick shift and clutch? But on icy mornings like this one, I sometimes considered buying a new one if the seats were heated.

I opened the door, crawled in, and turned the key in the ignition. A rumble. Cranked on the first try. I pressed on the gas pedal, slid the heater lever to high, got out, and left my faithful old wheels humming. So what if it was slow to heat up? It was old.

I'm getting old, and I'm slow to get going too. We're used to each other.

The phone was ringing when I walked through the kitchen door. "Yes, Susannah Hope. I'm dressed and waiting for the truck to get warm before I head to the church. Henrietta's having one last meeting before our trip. I think she just likes leading something."

"Just make her happy and let her lead. She's good at it. I was calling to see if you'd like to invite any of the ladies going on the trip to your goodbye luncheon on Thursday."

"Good grits and gravy, Susannah Hope, I don't need some goodbye luncheon. I'm not leaving for a year's tour of duty on the other side of the planet. I'm just going over to North Carolina for a week."

"I know, but I'm hosting lunch for Evie and Kate, and I thought I'd invite Laramie and her mom. Oh, and Lisa's out of school, so she can come. We'll make it a family Christmas luncheon for the ladies. Mindy and Laramie are like family now. We just want to give you a good send off."

"Well, it is a sweet thought, and it'll be good to have the hens together without the roosters, but I don't think we need any old biddies at this table. Besides, I'll be spending enough time with these ladies as it is. I'm not used to that much company, and frankly, I don't know if I'm ready for this or not."

"Now, Mama, check your attitude. You know how you used to talk to Diana Joy and me about that. If you start this trip with a good attitude, you'll have a lot more fun. It's fine if you don't want to invite your friends to lunch. They're probably busy the day before the trip anyway. I'll set the luncheon table for seven, and it'll just be family."

"Good. And you do the cookin'. Whatever you do, don't ask Evie to bring anything, you hear? Now Mindy's a pretty good cook if you want to ask her to bring a dish. What do you want me to bring?"

"Not a thing. I'll take care of lunch without anyone's help. You'd better get going. You shouldn't be late for your meeting."

"I'll be leaving as soon as the truck warms up, which might be next week. Love you. Bye."

I knew Susannah Hope meant well, but she was making way too much over my trip. And I wasn't certain that was going to do well with Kate. Nothing good would come from rubbing this in her sad little face. She was having a hard enough time as it was.

Warm or not, I climbed in my truck and plugged in my tape of Perry Como singing Christmas songs. I sang along with him all the way into town. Nobody could sing "White Christmas" like he could. I didn't know what I'd do when this tape wore out. Henrietta had said to bring some Christmas CDs for the trip, but I didn't have CDs. Nothing to play them on at the farm, and my guess was that fancy new church van wouldn't have an eight-track player.

Perry was good company on my way to town. I finished "White Christmas" before I got out of my truck, then walked down the church hallway to the Upper Room for our meeting. I could hear the guffawing when I rounded the corner. Henrietta met me at the door all dolled up in red pants and a red sweater with blinking Christmas lights around her neck. She handed me a bright-green envelope and told me where to sit. I couldn't believe all the trouble she had gone to for this meeting—music playing, place cards, and pictures of the Kentucky Castle and the Old Edwards Inn scattered over the top of the table.

I must have been the last to arrive because Henrietta followed me to my seat next to Roger Minton and then took her place at the head of the table and started her leading.

Carl Culpepper—eighty-two, strong, and the oldest of our traveling group—interrupted. "Henrietta, if you want me to hear what you're saying, turn off the music. I don't need "Jingle Bells" in my right ear and you in the other." Carl was normally quiet, but he didn't hesitate to speak up when something needed saying or doing. He'd been a deacon in our church for more than fifty years. "And you need to turn off the blinking Christmas lights around your neck. They're giving me a migraine."

Henrietta, her platinum hair sprayed stiff and her lips redder than her sweater and oily like she'd just eaten two pieces of bacon for breakfast, turned off the music. "Thank you, Carl. I'm just so excited that I forgot." She turned off her necklace, opened the green envelope in her hand, and started shuffling through pages. "As I was saying, I'm so glad we're all here this morning to go over the details of the trip. I can hardly wait until Friday. This is going to be the best Christmas trip ever, and with such a lovely group. We're a small one, but there's nothing wrong with that. Having only six of us will make our meals so simple and enjoyable. Not like that group of over thirty we took to Williamsburg last summer. Whew! That trip about did me in."

She looked over at me. "Why, Grace, I believe you're the only one who's never taken a trip with our XYZs! I'm here to tell you these folks know how to have a good time, and we're so glad you're joining us. Now, everybody, look in your green envelope, and let's go over things."

Henrietta led us through the packet, which included the itinerary, details of every day's activities, and every place where we would have a meal. There was a one-page map highlighting the routes we would take and bright red stars noting the places where we would stop along the way. Brochures from the Old Edwards Inn in Highlands and the Kentucky Castle in Lexington were in the green envelope.

My mind drifted as Henrietta gave descriptive details about the inn and the castle and the kinds of things we'd be doing there. I looked around the table at each of these folks like Joseph used to look at the pieces on his chess board, wondering what move to make. They would be my traveling family for Christmas. I had known them all for decades, but I had never spent Christmas with a one of them.

I'd known Carl Culpepper since I could remember. He owned a farm-equipment dealership, and Joseph had bought our tractor from him years ago when we built the farmhouse. For many years, those two had had early-morning coffee together at the café down the street from our hardware store before they went to work. They ate breakfast at home, but that cup of coffee with the guys had been a necessary start to their workday. All the folks around Cedar Falls respected Carl because he was an honest businessman and had helped so many of the young farmers get their start. His wife had died of cancer fifteen years ago, and Carl kept their home and still went to work every morning. Their two daughters lived away, but they came often with their children to check on Carl and spend time with him.

I glanced across the table at Rose Hadley. The folds in her leathery face and her high cheekbones bespoke her Native American ancestry. Her expression was peaceful, and lines of wisdom were deeply etched across her forehead. Rose had taught history and geography until she was forced to retire at age seventy-five. That was six years ago. The townsfolk were most unhappy about that. Hundreds of former students showed up for her retirement. My girls loved her and the way she had taught them about the world. Rose had a different way of looking at the world because she'd been to so many places. Some would call her a spinster because she'd never married. She might not have had children, but she had been like a mother to lots of kids in this community, inspiring them and helping them get a college education. The world travelers they were, she and

The Christmas Portrait Surprise

Evie have become quite good friends. They understood each other, I imagined.

Roger Minton sat next to me. He wasn't officially retired; he still spent a few hours at the bank most days. Lots of these old farmers and miners around these parts only wanted to do business with him. It had been a shame when that oil truck hit his wife head on. John had the first paramedic on the scene, but he'd said that she died on impact. That nearly did Roger in for a while, but his friends and the church kept his head above the waters that would have drowned him in grief. I knew that feeling too well. Still came in waves for me since my Joseph had died, but at least I'd had a little time to prepare. Roger didn't, and he didn't get to say goodbye. He was a fine gentleman and another good deacon.

And then there was Lottie Brownlee, the life of the party. Lottie was alone now that her husband had passed on, but both of her children were still here. She was a homemaker and one of the finest cooks in the county. I thought she must have won every county-fair blue ribbon at one time or another.

It had been my idea last year for Henrietta and Lottie to join me in our secret of making the church aware of needing to help the poor folks in our community. We got their attention with the painted messages we left around on the church walls. Vandals, they called us. But when we tore the page out of big Bible on the altar table, underlined in red a passage where Jesus talked about how to treat the poor, and taped it to the pulpit on Easter Sunday, it set the whole church on edge. So we decided to confess. At least the messages we painted got a fresh coat of paint on walls that needed painting, and it got us a committee to figure out how to get outside the church walls to help some folks that needed help in our community.

Never knew it could be so productive and so much fun to be mischievous. And what could they do to three well-meaning old ladies?

"Grace?"

I was a bit startled when I heard my name. Felt like I'd been caught again. I looked at Henrietta.

"Grace? You with us?"

"I'm still sitting here, aren't I?" I realized I had missed everything she said as I was thinking about my traveling companions and wondering what it would be like to spend my very first Christmas away from home.

Henrietta giggled. "I asked if you had any questions."

"Just need to know what time to be at the church Friday morning."

"I was just about to remind everyone of that. I think we've covered everything else. We should be here with our luggage at seven, and then we will be ready to pull out at seven thirty. Don't forget to bring snacks to share, preferably something homemade. Roger, you and Carl are exempt from the homemade part. That just means you'd better bring lots of chocolate—good chocolate. Any other questions?"

Rose quietly asked, "What are we doing for Matt? It's not every pastor that would spend a whole day driving us to Highlands."

Henrietta responded, "Yes, I should have told you. I put enough money in the price you're paying for the trip to give him and his sweet wife a gift card for two nights at the Kentucky Castle whenever they want to go. It didn't cost us that much, but I think it will mean so much to them. I apologize for not telling you sooner."

"That's a lovely expression of our gratitude," Rose said, "and I'm certain he could use a break from his work. Who doesn't like a couple of nights somewhere different?"

Henrietta began to wrap up. "That's why I chose to do this for them. Any more questions?" No one spoke up. "Well, then, let's get home and start packing."

"Wait, wait just a minute," Lottie squeaked as she pulled a giant Christmas bag from under the table. "I have something for y'all." She shook a folded, colorful silk scarf until it floated across the table and revealed brightly colored Christmas balls on a black background bordered in gold. "I made these for us to wear on our trip. It took me forever to find this fabric. Ladies, I made Christmas scarves for each of you. And don't worry, Carl and Roger. I made a tie for both of you out of the same fabric."

Henrietta clapped. Carl's eyes were rolling like mine. Rose accepted hers graciously, and Roger draped his tie around his neck, and said, "Well, Lottie, you just thought of everything."

Lottie giggled again. "I did, didn't I? Now we can wear these and keep up with other. Everyone will know we're all together."

All together. Yes, we would all be together apart from our families. This Christmas was going to be different.

———◆———

Tuesday afternoon

Kate

I heard the honking when I walked out the school door. There was Granny Grace, and her wheels were on the curb again. Chesler was already in the truck beside her, and the truck door was open. "Where's Evie? She was to pick us up."

Chesler answered, "Granny said she got stuck."

"Stuck in what?" I climbed in and slammed the door.

"I don't know. Ask Granny."

"I did ask Granny, and you answered." I knew my eyes were blaring and my forehead streak was turning red. "Granny, your wheels are up on the sidewalk again. One of these days, you're going to hurt somebody. And where's Evie?"

"Well, I haven't hurt anybody, and I haven't put a dent in anyone's car yet either. And to answer your question, Evie got stuck in her darkroom developing pictures and asked me if I could pick you up from school and take you to my house. Christmas rush for some of her clients. Your dad will come and get you before supper."

"Good." I zipped it. I didn't have anything else to say to Granny Grace.

Chesler piped up, "Granny, you got Christmas cookies? Or what about your fudge?"

I answered before she could. "No, Chesler, we made some stuff, and she took it to Aunt Susannah's because Granny's going away for Christmas. Why would she need cookies or fudge?"

Granny was driving slow today. "Seems you two have a problem with asking questions of me and then answering them before I can. Yes, Chesler, I do have some cookies and divinity. And my fudge with the white-chocolate peppermint bark—the kind we make every Christmas."

Chesler scooted next to Granny and hugged her. "Can you drive faster, Granny?"

Granny pushed in her Christmas tape, and she and Chesler sang all the way to the farm. I was quiet because I didn't have anything else to say. But when we got to Granny's, I slammed the truck door, the screen door, and the kitchen door as hard as I could. I tossed my backpack on the kitchen table where I knew Granny didn't like it to be.

She didn't say a word to me, but she handed Chesler a

cookie and said, "Ches, I know you've been building that fort in the loft in the barn, but I've been hearing some strange noises out there at night. And I think Sadie's been in there the last couple of days. You better go check to see if she's made a mess. Just be careful on the ladder."

Chesler flew out the back door, hollering, "Me and Sadie's gonna go 'round if she's been messin' in my fort."

Granny Grace looked at me. I watched her take a deep breath before she said, "Katherine Joy, you're quiet today, except your slamming doors said a lot. Maybe like you were yelling at me. I think you and I need to have a little talk, one like we've not had before. I know you're not happy with me and my decision to go away for Christmas."

I had my speech ready, and it was short. "Granny, what you're doing going away for Christmas is just plain wrong. And it's selfish. You need to listen to yourself, Granny. Like when you tell me, 'Kate, you're sufferin' from a case of yourself.' How many times have you told me that?" I stopped, but before Granny could answer, I started again. "I'm just tellin' you, Granny, you got a bad case of yourself. It's so bad you've given it to the rest of us. I hope you're happy about that and that you have a Merry Christmas." I stomped out before she could see me cry and went down the hall to the bathroom.

Once I was finished with the tears, I splashed water on my face and wiped my eyes. That gave Granny Grace time to dry her eyes too. I knew her eyes were teary when I walked away.

When I came back to the kitchen, she didn't say a word. She just hugged me. "I'm sorry, Kate that you're so angry. I promise you I did not make this decision to hurt your feelings. But you must respect my feelings, and I won't be changing my mind just because you're mad. And you must trust me that I truly don't have a bad case of myself. I have many reasons for my choice, and they're not all for me. We will have our Christmas, sweet girl. It will just be a few days late."

"No. It won't be Christmas." I cried hard into Granny's wool sweater, sniveling again in spite of myself. "It won't be Christmas without you, Granny Grace. It just won't be Christmas."

With that, I sat down at her breakfast table and got out my drawing pad and pencils. No more talking. No use.

Chapter Six

———— ♦ ————

Granny Grace

I allowed Kate to pout for a while. Maybe she deserved a good pout. I knew that mood, and it meant no talking when those drawing pencils were in her hand, but I finally broke the silence. "Looks like these gray clouds are setting in on us like a nesting hen on three eggs, but I sure had sun shining through this kitchen window this morning."

Kate didn't answer.

"Your granddad built this log house so the morning sun would shine on this kitchen, even in the winter when the sun moves south."

I thought talking about her granddad might get a rise out of her. She still didn't answer. She'd always been quiet like that when she was stewing about something. She'd say something when she was good and ready.

I watched her at the table sketching. Not intentionally drawing but nervously moving her pencil, smudging the charcoal on the paper, and mostly avoiding my question. I knew what my granddaughter was thinking, just like I knew what her mother was thinking when she was that age. And I knew Kate was drawing a redbird. She'd had a thing about redbirds ever since Diana Joy told her to always remember her when she saw one. Seemed kinda fitting since Diana Joy had the brightest red hair and could sing like a songbird too. Life had dealt Kate plenty of pain already, and there just might be more before it got better. "Kate?" I waited. "Katherine Joy, did you hear what I said?"

She ignored me, put down her pencil, reached inside the pouch I'd made for her, and picked up her eraser. That child used her eraser as much as she did the pencils. Said she was creating light and space.

Wish I had an eraser to take away her darkness.

"Katherine Joy, not talking about this won't change a thing, you know."

"You said talking about it won't change your mind, either, so I don't suppose there's any use in talking about it, is there?" Her nimble hand followed the eraser, circling and hovering over that paper like Grandpa Thatcher's divining rod over dry ground. She didn't even look up.

Sometimes that girl put strong periods at the ends of her sentences, but she'd talk sooner or later. "Don't you even want to know why I'm really going? Or maybe you just want me to tell Chesler. Then he can explain it to you after I leave." I knew that would get her. She'd been protective of her little brother since she took over her mother's role.

"Oh, just go, Granny Grace. Go on your old trip. I hate Christmas anyway."

Now anybody in Cedar Falls would tell you Grace O'Donnell's always had an opinion—sometimes informed, sometimes not, but nonetheless, an opinion. Right now, I decided it might be better if I kept my opinions to myself.

Think I'll make some hot chocolate. Maybe it'll go down

easier than what I got to say. Better put another log on the fire too.

Early snow was coming down, and if it stayed this cold, the kids would be out skating on the pond by Christmas Eve. I hated to miss that. Chesler was plum proud to pass down his outgrown skates to his little cousin, and I just imagined Chesler would be the one to hold Hank's hand when they got on the ice.

Susannah Hope had all but given up on having kids of her own when Baby Hank came along. That little copper-topped fellow had been a gift to all of us when he was born the year after Diana Joy died. And he must have primed the pump, because now there was another one on the way. Hoping for a girl, Susannah Hope had already named her Gracie. Some folks around this town might think there was just one too many Graces or Joys or Hopes in this family, but we liked it that way.

We'd always been big on Christmas too. I'd always been fond of the holiday. I'd been only one day old on my first Christmas. "This baby was born for Christmas," Papa had proudly announced. "Grace Noel's the proper name for any baby entering this world on Christmas Eve." Mama always said she was glad I was a girl. A boy named Grace Noel would have had a hard time surviving in a small Kentucky town.

I spent over fifty Christmases of my life right in the middle of town in the house where I was born, but fourteen years ago when Joseph sold the hardware store, we'd practically given that old Victorian house to Susannah Hope just to keep it in the family, and we built us this log house out in the country on Joseph's family place. I'd been tired of creaky stairs and narrow hallways and too many rooms without closets and plumbing that sounded like it was in pain.

And Joseph? Why he could hardly wait for the builders to get started so he'd have a dry place to construct the dining table he'd been waiting for years to build. He set up his sawhorses right here in this room because the table he was building would be too big to move in after the farmhouse was finished. The table was made out of four doors—two from our old house in town and two Joseph had salvaged from the house where he was born. They had the patina of two families' goings and comings for three generations. Joseph had said he wanted a dining table big enough for all the O'Donnells, so he worked his carpenter's magic putting those doors together, planing them down smooth and sealing them, and they'd been linking the generations of our family ever since.

When Joseph died six years ago, Susannah Hope and Diana Joy had insisted I move back to town, taking turns living with them. They thought it was unsafe for me to live out this far by myself. I couldn't sell them on the idea that my Winchester would take care of me, but they finally backed off when I told them I wasn't moving to town without my guineas and my goats. My farmhouse and the peace out here were just to my liking, and there had been enough laughing and crying and hugging and drinking coffee and eating macaroni and cheese in this place to make it home now.

We'd moved in the year little Katherine Joy was born, and she'd spent every Easter, Thanksgiving, and Christmas Eve of her life around this table, first in her mama's arms, then in the highchair Joseph built for her, and then in her own ladderback chair when she was tall enough to reach her plate.

Just something special about that first granddaughter. Now, Kate hadn't gotten her mama's red hair or her pretty singing voice, but she got Diana Joy's good heart and her love of making things. She'd taken her mama's dying pretty hard, and she was still a hair on the angry side, and I understood why. I'd had my parents until I was fifty. I'd had my husband for forty-six years, and I'd only lived in three houses my whole life. But this girl's life had been one change after the other. First her grandpa died, then her mama, and then John married to Evie.

Evie had showed up the first Christmas after Diana Joy died. She was here to visit her brother, our pastor. Pastor Simmons had buried Joseph and Diana Joy and baptized the grandchildren, so he was already part of this clan. And Kate had liked Evie well enough. After all, when Kate met Evie and learned she was a photojournalist, she made friends fast. Kate was always interested in anything that captured a face on paper, be it a drawing pencil, a paint brush, or a camera. Evie settled down here and opened a small gallery.

It took John a while to get used to the idea of loving Evie. But I'd had an O'Donnell sense about this from the start. She was good for John and the kids, and Diana Joy would have liked her a lot. John needed a wife, and the Lord knew Kate and Chesler needed a Mama. I was getting old, and I had a bad ticker. But now Kate would have Evie and a chance at seeing the world that I only dreamed about.

I'd been saving the chunk of chocolate Evie brought me from her last assignment in Africa. I let Kate be silent until I sat down with two mugs of rich, dark hot chocolate and a fresh bag of marshmallows. "Here, Kate, this'll warm your bones." Her glassy eyes, about to spill out tears, met mine just as I removed the pencil from her hand. "Time for silence is over, sweet girl. Time for talking now."

"No use talking, Granny Grace. You said so yourself it won't change things. You're going no matter what I say." She didn't reach for the marshmallows or her cup. Her body sat still like when her mama had died. Like if she moved, she might crack and tears would start to flow and she couldn't be put back together again.

"That's right, Kate. That's what I said. But sometimes talking things out's a lot like praying. Might not change a thing but the one who's praying. And most of the time, that's what's needed anyhow. So you're right, talking won't keep me from going, but it'll help you understand why I need to go."

She raised her voice. "You know what you always say about the difference between needing and wanting. You don't need to go, Granny. You just want to. Why?"

Neither of us had even tasted the hot chocolate, and I didn't find it easy being flogged with my own words. "Okay, you drink your cocoa and let me explain." I took a sip myself. Maybe that warm, silky chocolate would sweeten my words.

"You know, some of these folks who are making the trip don't have anyone to be with at Christmas. Like Miss Rose Hadley. Why, she doesn't even have a family. So she'll leave home, lock the door on her loneliness, and celebrate Christmas with us friends in a castle. And there are some in the group who've lost their loved ones. Including me. So when Henrietta invited me to go, I said yes. I've never spent Christmas in a castle before."

"But you have family, and you'd rather say no to us? You'd just rather leave us alone at Christmas and go off to some castle with strangers. That's just plain wrong, Granny."

"Now, just wait a minute. These folks are not strangers. I've known most of them all my life. That's a lot longer than I've known you." I took another sip. "And just who is it that'll be alone at Christmas if I'm not here? Not you. You have your daddy and Evie and Chesler, and your Aunt Susannah Hope and her clan. So tell me again, Kate, who's going to be alone?"

"But Granny, there's nobody to make the French onion soup and the special grilled cheese sandwiches and the cookies we always have on Christmas Eve. You know Aunt Susannah Hope always skimps on the cheese, and she just hates cutting up onions. And Evie can't cook. She only opens cans. And we won't get to sign the Christmas tablecloth. And I already taught Baby Hank how to write an *H* so he could sign it this year for the first time. It's our tradition, Granny."

Kate had always loved the family Christmas tablecloth, and I'd promised it to her when I went to heaven. "Kate, did you ever think it might be time to start some new traditions? We need to consider Evie. She's new to the family, and maybe she has some of her own traditions."

She pushed the mug of hot chocolate away. "Well, we don't have to give up our traditions just so she can have hers."

When God rationed out stubborn, Kate got more than her share, but thank the Lord, she got her share of smarts too. "So, now, let me make sure I understand this. Evie's supposed to give up her family traditions because she's part of our family now?" I swirled the hot chocolate in my cup and let her ponder that for a spell. "Is that what you're planning to do when you get married? Give up your traditions, like our family Christmas Eve tablecloth and onion soup and grilled cheese sandwiches, just because you're marrying into some lucky young man's family? Did I get that right?"

Kate finally reached for her hot chocolate. I figured she needed a sip or two to buy herself some time to respond. "You're just being selfish. If you're gone, it won't be the same. Nobody else knows how to make the cinnamon buns for Christmas morning."

Like I said, smart granddaughter I have, dodging my question like that. "Well, you might as well get used to missing those traditions if you have to give them up when you marry into another family."

She reached for her pencil again, but I covered her hand with mine. "Look, Kate. Being family is sort of like making this hot chocolate. I could have given you a mug of warm, sweet milk, and that would have been just fine. Or I could have given you a chocolate bar for your snack and that would have been fine too. But when I put the two together, we got hot chocolate. The milk didn't quit being milk. It's just sweeter and richer. And the chocolate didn't quit being chocolate, it just melted into that warm milk and made it pretty tasty, wouldn't you say?"

She reached for her mug again. I gave her time to sip. "That's what being family is, Kate. Blending folks' lives together to make a new family. And no matter what I do, I can't separate this chocolate from the milk and from the sugar and from those marshmallows that melted on top, just like a family melting together, adding and blending traditions."

"You still don't have to go, Granny."

"Yes, I do, child. As long as I'm here running things, Evie won't feel free to put her fingerprint on Christmas, and she deserves that. Think about it, Kate. I've had my turn, and your mama did too. And what we started won't all go away, it'll just get added to."

Kate stood straight up from where she was sitting at the end of the table. "Why do you have to be nice to Evie and not to the rest of us? You're saying these things, but you're really just being mean and selfish. And I don't think you really want to go. You might as well stop talking, Granny, 'cause I'm not listening anymore." She put her drawing pencils and the eraser in the pouch, tied the closure, and crumpled the paper and left it on the table as she rounded the corner where I had my suitcase ready for packing. I turned just in time to see her kick it. That wasn't so much like Kate, but I guess she deserves to kick something.

I smoothed out the crinkled paper to see the redbird she had drawn—the redbird sitting in the bare sycamore tree next to the barn. The sound of the siren in the squad car let me and the guineas know John was coming up the hill. John did that for Chesler sometimes since there was nobody out this way to hear it but me and the Hortons down the lane. But they were used to it.

Chesler came running to the house and gave me a good-bye hug and ran out the back door again. John said, "I'll go make certain the guineas are back in the barn for the night and close the door. I know those poor hens scatter to their hiding places when they hear the siren."

Kate lingered at the back door while her dad took care of the guineas and getting Chesler in the truck. She was a kind and thoughtful child, and I knew she was having a hard time leaving angry. Her eyes were fixed on the redbird in the sycamore tree.

I put my arm around her. She stiffened, turned, and looked straight at me. "You're right, Granny. You can't take the chocolate back out of the hot chocolate. But you sure can pour it all down the drain, and that's what you're doing leaving your family at Christmas. You don't have to go, Granny Grace."

I hugged her, feeling the softness of her hair against my leathery old cheek. "Yes, I do, child. And one day, you'll understand why."

Chapter Seven

———— ♦ ————

Tuesday night, December 17
Cedar Falls

Granny Grace

The house was quiet again, and after a bowl of leftover potato soup, I was quite ready to settle in. I fixed myself a cup of chamomile tea, stood in front of the fire, and looked out the large window to see if the gray had given way to the sun's last rays on the horizon. When we built this place, Joseph hadn't cared where we put anything except the windows. He wanted to catch the early morning light and the sunsets. No stale, lace curtains or shades on any window in this house.

I pulled my favorite rocker a bit closer to the hearth and sat down to warm my feet and closed my eyes. The fire was crackling, and the wind hummed me to sleep. Next thing I knew, the phone was ringing, and I nearly spilled cold tea on myself trying to answer it. Nobody ever called this late except John if he needed help with the children.

It was John all right. No emergency but a problem nonetheless. "You're going to have to help me out here, Grace. Kate's really upset about your leaving, and I don't know what else to say to her. She's blaming Evie, and now she's got Chesler in on it too. He thinks you're going away to die just like the old Indian chief did in a movie we watched a couple of Saturdays ago."

I listened for a spell as John rattled on. "John, you have to tell the kids I'm going because I want to go. You already know that I have lots of reasons for going. Remind them I have friends just like they do. And tell Chesler I'll call every night so he won't think I've wandered off to some ancient Indian burial ground." I got quiet. "I'm sorry Evie's getting the brunt of this. I never meant for that to happen."

"She's handling it okay. She's just amazing."

"And Kate and Chesler will be fine too. This will be over, and they will survive."

"I know. If you have any other bright ideas, let me know. And I'll be out to pick you up early Friday morning and deliver you to the church."

We parted for the night. I hated those kids had to learn so young about grief and how quickly life can change. Like with their grandpa. One minute he had picked up his hat and headed to the barn, and the next minute he had collapsed in the shed and was hollering for help. We had planted tulip bulbs that morning, and his body was at Park's Funeral Home that afternoon. Kate cried and cried because she didn't get to say goodbye.

And then a few months later, Diana Joy got cancer and died at home with Kate beside her, holding her hand.

Losing someone you love was not easy no matter how old or young you were. I just didn't want her to grow up afraid of loving somebody for fear of losing them.

Joseph had been gone for a while, and I still missed him, mostly early in the morning when I woke up and then late in the afternoon when the sun was slipping away. And some late evenings, I sat right here when the last embers were mostly gray ash, and I looked at his empty chair, and as if he were still sitting there, I talked to him about my day.

I wasn't sure what he'd think about the Christmas tree not being in the corner, but he'd probably have plenty to say about the Christmas tablecloth not being on the family table this year. That white linen cloth had been on the O'Donnell Christmas table since the first year we were married. It had been a gift from Joseph's mother, and she nearly got the vapors when I brought red and green markers to the table and we signed our names and the date right in the middle. And every Christmas since, we'd been signing that cloth. It was covered in stains and memories. Said a whole lot about our family—Susannah Hope's perfectly formed letters on an invisible straight line and Diana Joy's playful letters, different sizes and colors. She even wrote her name and message backward one year just for fun and pulled out a mirror so we could read it. Joseph's signature never changed in forty-three years—green block letters, all capital.

And now the next generation was leaving its mark on the Christmas cloth. The first Christmas without Diana Joy, Kate had drawn a picture of a redbird and put her mama's name under it. Her green eyes searched for that bird every Christmas when we spread the cloth on the table, and she managed to sit where the redbird appeared.

I got up and closed the doors on the fireplace and looked out the window at the sliver of moon over the pond. Snow was still falling. I remembered what Joseph had told Susannah Hope when she insisted we put up shades on the windows. He said very matter-of-factly, "I put that window right where it is so the evening sun would shine through it. Your mama and I have worked all our lives and missed too many sunsets with all our busyness, but we'll not miss another one. We're through drawing curtains and pulling shades. We'll just wait on the Good Lord to pull down the night sky over the sunset."

———•———

Wednesday morning, December 18

When I heard Henrietta's voice on the phone, I knew to sit down. "No, Henrietta, I have not finished packing. I'm standing here looking at the stacks on my bed, and it looks like Sadie's been in here."

"Sadie? Who's Sadie?"

"Just the most cantankerous old guinea I've got. Shows up in some surprising places and leaves a mess and tears up stuff everywhere she goes. All the clothes on my bed look like she's been in here trying to make a nest."

I heard Henrietta chuckle, but I didn't join her. "Well, I'm glad you can laugh about my predicament. Honestly, Henrietta, I'm not like you. You're always sittin' on *G*, waitin' on *O*, and then you're off again. Why, it's been so long since I've made a trip, I don't even know where to begin to pack. From the looks of what's stacked on my bed, I could stay in Highlands for the rest of the winter."

"Stop, what you're doing, Grace. I'll be there in twenty minutes with my packing list. I'll help you. I'm a packing expert."

"You don't need to do that. Surely I have sense enough to put some clothes in a suitcase."

"Well, if you won't let me come . . . Look, go pour yourself another cup of coffee and sit down with a pad and pencil and make columns for every day that we'll be gone. You have the itinerary and know what we'll be doing every day. So write down what you're going to wear each day. Just make sure your clothes are warm and that you have comfortable shoes. Then make another list of the things you'll need every day, things like your medicine and toiletries and underwear and nightgown. Oh, and don't forget accessories. You know, like scarves and jewelry and one of your knitted hats. And for sure pack something that looks holiday-ish. Put it all on the list, and then put the stuff on the list in your luggage."

"You and your lists sound like my daughter Diana Joy. I still have the lists she made for me before she went to heaven. I guess she got that from her daddy. She didn't get it from me. I prefer doin' over list makin'."

"Trust me, Grace. I promise you this list will save you some frustration. And don't forget we have two dressy nights. So you'll need evening clothes. And for goodness' sake, pack your jewelry. I packed mine once in my velvet bag and put that bag back in the drawer until the day I was supposed to leave, and I forgot it. I felt naked that whole trip without my jewelry. Oh, and shoes. You have to have shoes and bags to match your outfits."

"You mean I can leave my barn jacket and work boots at home but take my rubies and my ruby slippers?"

"That does it, Grace. I couldn't get you to my dress shop to buy some new things, so I'm on my way. I'm not having you embarrass yourself and me on this trip. Besides, I think Roger has taken a liking to you, and I intend to see that you look fabulous and behave on this trip. He may be checking you out."

"Henrietta, I don't think you're up to that. At least not the making me behave part." I was glad she couldn't see my eyes rolling. "Just go on back to what you were doing. I gotta go, and if I have any questions, I'll call you. Bye." I wasn't about to let that conversation continue or else I might change my mind about taking this trip, but she quickly started again.

"Actually, I was thinking maybe you shouldn't behave,

just this once. We had fun misbehaving last Easter. And I'll make sure you look fabulous. I'll do your makeup. I think you've forgotten how since Joseph died." Henrietta paused, but I could hear her snorting like she did when she was nervous. "Now, Grace, I'm about to say something. You know I love you and I don't want to hurt your feelings, but I'm just going to say it. You need to go and get your hair done."

"What do you mean get my hair done? I do my hair every day."

"No, I mean really done. I'll call my girl and get you an appointment. I'll tell her what to do, and she'll give you a short cut and color."

"Henrietta, I'm at the end of my sixth decade, and I've worn long hair all my life. I've never colored it. I brush it and braid it down the back and pile it on top of my head. I don't care much about hair. I do my own, and I wouldn't know what to do with short hair. And besides, what color do you want it?"

"Well, your hair was beautiful when you were young, and it was that deep auburn color. But now . . . Grace, it looks like the color of something your guinea—what was her name? Sadie? It just looks like something Sadie would make a nest out of. At least go and get a trim and let my hairdresser condition it. We're going on a nice trip, and you never know what might happen."

"Whatever happens, my hair's going to look just like it does this morning, I'll have you know. Although, I may put a Christmas ribbon in it or one of your stupid-looking blinking Christmas-light necklaces twined around in my braid. I could do that."

"Now, Grace, you're mad. I know you are. I'm sorry. What can I say to make it better? We need to make up. I mean we're going to be seat mates on a van for eight days, and we'll be sharing a room for seven nights."

No way to be mad with Henrietta long. She couldn't help being a dressed-up, painted-up little fire hydrant, spewing and spraying everywhere she went. Most of the time she was fun, but she surely could make my eyes roll. We'd been friends since grade school, and I knew she meant well. "I'll tell you how you can make up with me. You take Roger for yourself. I have zero, zilch—that means *no*—interest in Roger. I'm hanging up now to do what you told me to do. I'll make a list and pack, but that's all, you hear? Bye for now. If I think of something, I'll call you."

I hung up the phone before Henrietta could say another word and took her advice and sat down with another cup of coffee to make my list. When it was finished and my cup was empty—and not just my coffee cup—I felt a hollowness where my heart used to be. I wouldn't be home for Christmas. I was upset about it, I had upset Kate, and now I had upset Henrietta.

I sat there with my arms propped on the table and held my head in my hands. I closed my eyes and prayed. "Lord, am I doing the right thing? I don't seem to know anymore. If I had my way, my whole family would be here for Christmas. I'd be getting the house ready and all the food prepared, and I'd be looking forward to the Christmas Eve service and Christmas morning with the children. But that's not what our Christmas celebration is anymore. Joseph and Diana Joy are in heaven with You, and sometimes I feel closer to heaven than I do to where I am. I miss them so much. I'm still here doing what I thought was best for this family, but I'm not as sure about this trip as I was when I decided to go. I've been the take-charge one and the glue to hold them together too long. Susannah Hope's learning to step up, and John and Evie are trying to build a life. Sometimes I think I'm just in the way, and then I look into little Katherine Joy's eyes. I don't know if I see her or Diana Joy.

"Lord, how I hope I haven't made a mess of things by making this trip. Just give me strength to go through with it, and please bring some joy to Kate. I don't expect her to understand, just like she still doesn't understand why her mama died. She's got to learn to trust You, Lord. I know You can make something good out of this mess, and I sure hope You will. Amen."

My burden hopefully lessened, I sat up with a sigh. *Need to get to it. I'm going away for Christmas. Shouldn't take too long to pack my suitcase now with this list.*

————•————

Wednesday night

Kate

At the supper table, Chesler told us all about the fort he was building in the loft in Granny's barn. He was jumping-up-and-down happy when Daddy told him there was an old tarp and stakes in the garage and explained how he could use them. They took off to the garage as soon as their plates were clean. Laramie and I helped Evie clear the table.

Laramie was using her manners. "Mrs. Harding, that spaghetti was so good, and I really liked all that fresh Parmesan cheese on it."

I watched the smile spread on Evie's face. I had to give her that. She had learned to make spaghetti, and we had it a lot.

"Why, thank you, Laramie. And if it's all right with you, why don't you just call me Evie like Kate does? I do love hearing 'Mrs. Harding,' but you're family, and 'Mrs.

Harding' seems a bit formal."

Laramie shook her head. "Thank you, but I don't know if my mom would like it if I did that."

"Then I'll just ask her, and you're a smart girl to think of such." Then Evie looked at me. "Do you want to watch a Christmas movie, or do you girls have other plans that don't include the rest of the family?"

Laramie's look nudged me to answer. "We can watch a movie if you'd like to. I have a project Laramie's going to help me with, but we have all day tomorrow."

I saw Evie's raised eyebrows. "Did you forget? We're all having lunch over at Susannah's tomorrow. It's a sendoff for Granny Grace."

"I didn't forget, but I'm not going."

I felt Laramie's stare. She's got a stare like nobody else. "Kate, you gotta go. My mom and I are invited to be part of your family tomorrow. My mom's really looking forward to it, and she's taking a special dish. Granny Grace is going to love it."

"Well, then, you can go. I don't want to go to some goodbye luncheon for Granny."

Evie interrupted. "I'm sorry you're unhappy with Granny Grace right now, but it would disappoint everyone if you didn't fill your place at the table."

"You mean like how Granny's disappointing everybody because she won't be here for Christmas Eve, and Christmas morning breakfast, and for opening the presents, and then for Christmas dinner? It's okay with everyone if she's not here to fill her place at the table, but it's not okay if I miss some ol' luncheon. I don't get that."

"Your aunt Susannah Hope is just trying to do something nice for all of us, especially your grandmother. And Kate, you must go. You can't disappoint everyone."

"I'll think about it, but I'm not promising."

"Kate, I don't recall asking you to think about it, and you don't need to promise anything, because this is not one of those times when you get to decide. You've been taught to do what is right, and your dad and I would not be very responsible adults if we allowed you to choose to do the wrong thing in this situation. We're all expecting you to be there and to be pleasant and not to call attention to yourself. This is for Granny Grace, and Susannah Hope is going to a lot of trouble."

I knew Evie was right, but I still didn't like it. "You're making me go?"

"I hope making you go won't be necessary. I want you to think about how much Granny does for this family every day, and how much we love her. Don't forget how much she misses your mom and your granddad. And now she wants to do this one thing for herself. Maybe if you thought it about it that way, you wouldn't be so angry, and you would choose to be there for lunch."

"Since I have no choice, I'll go." I grabbed Laramie's arm and started out of the kitchen. "Come on, Laramie." I turned around to Evie. "Do we have to watch some ol' Christmas movie too?"

"No, Kate. That's your choice."

"Then we won't. We'll be up in my room."

"That's fine, but maybe before you go upstairs, you and I should apologize to Laramie for our behavior. It's not very gracious of us to have this kind of conversation in front of her when she's your guest." Evie waited, but I said nothing, so Evie spoke first. "Laramie, I'm sorry if our conversation made you uncomfortable."

"Oh, no, ma'am. It's okay. I know about having conversations with my mom and my dad. I understand. Kate's thinks she's mad, but she's just sad, and she doesn't want Granny Grace to take this trip. But she'll think about it, and she'll stop pouting and be okay."

Then I felt Laramie giving me the stare again, and her arm went around my shoulders.

"Come on, Kate, we'll go upstairs, and you can be mad on me and get it all over with. And then tomorrow, you'll be Kate again."

I still didn't say a word, but Evie answered. "Thank you, Laramie. You and Kate are like sisters. We're so glad to have you around. Now go on upstairs. I'm about to watch the movie all by myself. We have snacks if you girls get hungry."

I stomped up the stairs and slammed the door to my room, but Laramie caught the door before it made a sound. I walked over to my bed and sat down. "So, you're taking Evie's side. I thought you were my friend."

Laramie walked over in front of me. "I am your friend. I was just trying to be nice to Evie. And besides, I wouldn't be much of a friend if I wasn't honest with you."

"Then if you're my friend, prove it. You have to help me. I've made up my mind. I'm going to do what you did. You ran away. That really got your dad's attention, and he started doing better, and your mom came home. And y'all had the best Christmas. If I run away tomorrow night and everybody thinks I'm missing, Granny won't go. I would just have to be gone one night because they're leaving Friday morning. I would come home after the others left on their trip so nobody has to worry long. Then Granny would be here for Christmas."

Laramie pointed her finger in my face. "That's crazy, Kate. My mom was in rehab, but I didn't know it. I was living alone with my dad, and he hit me. I was scared to stay there. That's why I ran away. And you do remember it was in a snowstorm? I've never been so scared in my whole life."

"It's not snowing much yet, and I was kinda thinking I could come stay at your house for that one night. I could sneak in your bedroom window after your parents go to sleep, and then I could leave early Friday morning. I still have to figure out where I can hide in the daytime until it's safe to come home and Granny's here."

"This is getting even crazier. You're going to be in so much trouble, and now you're trying to drag me into it." Laramie walked across the room and stared out the window. That was better than her staring at me.

"It's the only thing I can think of to keep Granny here for Christmas. If you won't help me run away, do you have any other ideas?"

"Yeah, what about just forgetting about it? Let Granny Grace go and enjoy herself with her friends."

I primped up to cry. "It's not all about me, Laramie. I know that's what you and Evie think, but Granny doesn't really want to go. She wants to be here. I know she does."

I heard a bump at the door, but then it stopped.

Laramie turned and looked at me. "If she doesn't want to go on this trip, and you don't want her to go, then why is she going?"

"She's got some crazy kind of notion that we need to have our own Christmas without her." I wiped my tears on my sweater sleeve.

"You mean like she's preparing you for when she goes to heaven like your mom did?"

"Maybe. I'm not sure. That's what Chesler thinks."

"Is that what she said?" Laramie came over to my desk, pulled out the desk chair, and sat down in front of me.

"Not exactly, but she said enough to make me think she wants Evie and all of us to start doing Christmas a new way. And Granny thinks the only way we'll do that is if she's not here."

"I thought you were just being selfish, but you're trying to rescue Granny too. I'm sorry for sounding mean. But

Kate, you have to promise me—I mean, really promise me—that you won't run away."

Just when Laramie said that, Chesler came bumbling into my room. "Kate, are you runnin' away?"

I yanked his arm and pulled him down to sit next to me, and Laramie got up to close the door. "So you've been sneakin' again. How long have you been listening? What did you hear?"

"I heard Laramie say you were runnin' away."

"Well, I'm not runnin' away. You misunderstood 'cause you didn't hear it all. I just feel like runnin' away 'cause I'm sad that Granny won't be here for Christmas. I thought about it, but it's a dumb idea. So you'd better not say a word."

"You mean if you ran away, Granny wouldn't go on her trip?"

"Like I said, Chesler, it was a dumb idea. And if you say one word about this to Daddy or Evie, I will tell Daddy that you were the one who got into his tackle box. And you know what that means. Do you understand?"

"I didn't mess it up. I just got some fishin' line. And you're not gonna run away. I'm not sayin' nothin', Kate. Nothin'."

"You'd better not. Now get outta here, and stay outta my room. And quit sneakin'. Go back downstairs. Laramie and I are working on a Christmas project. It's a secret."

Chesler left my room and closed the door.

Laramie gave me the stare. "I got a bad feeling about this."

Chapter Eight

———— ◆ ————

Thursday morning, December 19
Cedar Falls

Granny Grace

I locked the back door, walked to Evie's car, and glanced at the empty back seat as I got in. "Why, Evie, you're looking absolutely lovely this morning. I should have borrowed that Christmas sweater for my trip."

"You can still borrow it."

"Thank you, but I think I have everything I need. I do appreciate your being my chauffeur for the luncheon. I know it was a special trip and out of your way."

"Oh, Grace, it's only three miles, and I do love this beautiful drive in the countryside."

"After all these years, I still enjoy the drive myself, especially if I'm coming home. Bless John's heart, he knew my old truck heater is close to breathing its last breath of warm air, and he and his buddy picked it up and took it to the shop yesterday afternoon. Maybe by the time I get back home, I'll be driving around in a sauna."

"That sounds inviting on a cold morning like this one. You can take me for a ride the next time. And you're right.

John is the best."

"He's like a son to me, and I'm glad you don't mind. I see Kate and Laramie aren't with you. Kate still got the mullygrubs this morning?"

"She's still pouting a bit, but she and Laramie were in the kitchen finishing up the strawberry salad when I left. Kate sent me to the grocery store early this morning for everything she needed. Mindy's picking them up and bringing them to Susannah's. They worked last night on some Christmas-gift projects. I had no idea when I married into this family that homemade Christmas gifts are the ones everyone expects, but I'm learning, and I cherish the idea."

"One of those family things. I heard the kids gave you the ornaments they made for you. That's a family thing too. We do take care of one another, just like you giving me a ride this morning. Susannah Hope won't have to worry about my running over her shrubbery again."

I looked out the car window to see the eastern hemlocks lining the lane. Their needles were covered with heavy frost. I wondered how many wreaths I had made from hemlock branches and how many layered strawberry salads Diana Joy had made. "So Kate's making the strawberry layered salad, is she?"

"If you can call it that. Sounds more like dessert to me with a pretzel crust, Jell-O, frozen strawberries, cream cheese, and whipped topping."

"Oh, that was Diana Joy's favorite, and she made it every Christmas. I've been making it for Kate since her mama wasn't here to make it for her. I'm surprised. I didn't know Kate knew how to make it."

"Honestly, I'm not sure that she does, and I wasn't much help. But Laramie called Mindy, and I think she walked them through it. I have so much to learn about this whole cooking thing as well as the handmade presents."

The Christmas Portrait Surprise

We passed by the winterberry bushes that grew on the fence line. Still had plenty of berries on all the branches. The birds would get every berry this winter because I wouldn't be cutting them for decorating. "You'll get the hang of it all. Not sure Kate cares how the strawberry salad turns out. It's her way of making a statement. Maybe more than one. She's still angry with me and echoing the words I've spoken to her at times. Told me Tuesday afternoon I had a bad case of myself."

"For sure she's not happy with you, but she'll get over it when you return and we have another reason to celebrate Christmas."

"I suppose."

"The good news is Chesler's not pouting. He's so excited about coming with me to bring you home this afternoon. John gave him an old tarp and some things for the fort he's building in the loft in your barn. He even outfitted some old tackle box as a toolbox for him. And Chesler wants to show me how to gather the eggs and feed the guineas while you're gone."

"Oh, I'm glad you mentioned eggs. I forgot to tell you. You remember Cecil Horton, Kate's classmate that lives down the lane? He'll be taking care of those chores. I'm thinking that his family needs the eggs, and I'm paying Cecil a bit to come and gather the eggs and water and feed the guineas. I figure he could use a little money, and it would save you from having to come out here every day. You know my hens. They're faithful layers, even in the wintertime in that warm coop, and those eggs will need gathering sometimes twice a day."

"We certainly don't mind coming out here, but that's a great idea. I'm sure the Hortons will appreciate the eggs, and it gives Cecil something to do while school's out for the holidays. We'll come out and check on things a couple of times to make sure he's responsible."

"Sounds good, but I can tell you, that boy is responsible. I've used him a few times to help me out with some chores around here—raking and mowing and stuff—and I'm impressed with that young man. His family doesn't have much, but they have integrity and good work ethics. They've just had some bad luck, but I'm grateful to the good Lord they're doing better these days. After that last baby was born, and the Biscuit Boys from the church repaired that house, and Mindy and I painted it and spruced it up, they've been doing better. Mr. Horton got a job as a truck driver, so he's home more than he used to be. They're coming to church too."

"Glad to hear that. I know you were largely responsible."

"Oh, not so much. The good Lord provided lots of help."

"Got your packing done?"

"I think so, except for the last-minute things. You and Henrietta are these perpetual travelers and know how to pack. But I haven't been away from home in years, so packing was an experience. Amazing that I got everything into one suitcase and a garment bag. Henrietta shared some tips with me that helped."

"I'm sure you'll have everything you need, and if you don't, just have a fun shopping spree. So often the places where I travelled in Africa and South America were not quite so civilized, and shopping was not convenient. Those experiences taught me about smart packing, and I learned to do without. Found out there are lots of things we think we need that we don't." Evie slowed as she drove into Susannah Hope's driveway.

"I know that's so." I pulled my jacket a bit tighter around myself and opened the car door. "Let's get this over with."

The Christmas Portrait Surprise

"Grace! You sound like Kate, like you're both going to the dentist. This will be a lovely luncheon, and you'll enjoy it. You do love being with your girls."

Evie was right about that. "I love being with them when we're all in a good mood, but I have a feeling the mullygrubs have crept into our Christmas."

In a matter of minutes, we were all around the table, and I was right about the mullygrubs. But oh, Susannah Hope had outdone herself with lunch, down to the white candles and white roses and holly in the centerpiece. She'd made a special kale salad to go with her lentil soup, and Mindy brought a pull-apart cheese bread varnished with melted butter. And right in the middle of the table on a silver tray sat Kate's strawberry salad.

"Mindy, I hope you'll give me this bread recipe. Goodness, you could open a bakery with this stuff, and maybe Kate could go into business with you with her salad. I'm so glad you remembered it and that you know how to make it."

I watched every tense muscle in Kate's sweet face.

"I won't ever forget. I used to help Mama make it every Christmas. I always crushed the pretzels for her." Kate paused. "See, Granny, we can do lots of things for ourselves for Christmas."

"I know you can, sweet girl. I never doubted it."

"So you really don't have to make your trip just so we learn to do things without you."

Susannah Hope nearly choked on her kale and tomatoes. "Excuse me, Katherine Joy. I don't think that's why she's going on this trip. We should be excited that she'll be celebrating with her friends in such lovely places. And we'll be celebrating as family just like we always do."

I watched Kate staring at her plate. Her tone was not sassy but almost resigned. "Not true. We always had

Christmas Eve at Granny's after church, never at your house. And Granny always made the cinnamon buns for Christmas morning at our house."

Susannah Hope responded quickly, "And we're having cinnamon buns just like always at your house. I'm making them. Evie and I have everything planned."

Kate was quiet on the outside, but I sensed a blusteriness inside her, maybe because I felt the same way. "Katherine Joy, I know this Christmas will be a little different, but we've had some practice the last few years adjusting to Christmas being different. I think that's the way of life, not just for our family but for everybody. We have our traditions, and we'll hang on to some of them and make some new ones. Let's try to keep our focus on the reason for our celebration, not just on our traditions. We'll all still be celebrating Jesus's birth no matter where we are, and we'll have another family celebration when I get home."

Things were quiet. No one rescued me, so I kept talking. "Have you put out the nativity scene yet? You know, the wooden one Chesler can't break?"

Kate never looked up. "It's on the hearth where we always have it, and Ches and I've been lighting the candle every night. I watch him so he's careful with the matches."

Mindy added to the conversation, "Oh, I wish you could see our nativity scene. My dad made us a wooden one in his workshop and gave it to us at Thanksgiving. Laramie did such a beautiful job of painting each piece. It has become a family treasure."

Evie responded, "Yes, we do have our treasures. In all of my travels as a photojournalist, I collected nativity scenes. Gave several of them to Matt for use at the church or with his family. Kate, what about you and Chesler going through those boxes in the storage unit with me and let's find them? Maybe we can decide on a place and put them out so we can enjoy them. But let me warn you, they don't all look like the ones you're used to. What do you think, Kate?"

Kate finally looked up at Evie. "Fine, if that's what you want to do."

Evie smiled slightly. "Maybe this could be a new tradition, and you could choose where we put them."

Susannah Hope blurted out, "I think that's a grand idea. Let's take the positive approach and get excited about making some new traditions and some beautiful new memories to go with our old ones."

Mindy added, "We're doing something different this year too. We're going to Virginia to my sister's house for Christmas. Laramie will see her cousins that she hasn't seen in a while."

I noticed the surprise on Kate's face. Another change. I'd be gone for Christmas and so would her best friend. But I trusted John and Evie and Susannah Hope.

They'll make sure Kate has a fine Christmas.

———•———

Thursday afternoon

Kate

I didn't have a choice. Evie said I needed to go with her and Chesler to take Granny Grace home. It'd be the last time we saw Granny until she got home from her trip. Evie and Granny were chattering away about the rooms and food at the Kentucky Castle. I mostly stared out the car window while Chesler went through the toolbox Daddy had made for him, taking everything out and laying it on the car seat, and then putting it all back in. It was just an old tackle box that had a screwdriver, a hammer, pliers, some nails and screws, and a tape measurer. I didn't know what Daddy was thinking. All that was just one big accident in Chesler's hands. At least he didn't give him a drill or a saw.

I saw Cecil and Sugar walking down the lane as we drove into Granny's driveway. Probably they were headed home. Evie tooted the horn, and they waved. Looked like they had a basket of pinecones and hemlock branches. Mrs. Horton was probably decorating like Granny used to, with the pine and the berries.

Every Christmas Mama and Granny Grace had gathered boxes of pinecones and sprayed them silver and gold. They'd cut them up and made wreaths out of them, stacked the pinecones up like a Christmas tree, and filled a big basket with them and put it next to the fireplace. Granny always tied a big red ribbon on the handle of the basket. Mama said it was those little touches that just made Christmas. But no dressing up Granny's house this year. Her farmhouse didn't look like Christmas. It didn't smell like Christmas, and it wouldn't sound like Christmas this year.

Evie parked the car, and Chesler grabbed his toolbox, opened the door, and jumped out like he had been ejected. When he did, his tools went everywhere, and he started hollering like they were all in pain. I got out to help him. "I told you to make sure the latch on that box was fastened. You never listen."

It took about thirty seconds to cram the tools in the box, and then he was off running to the barn, dragging the tarp behind him. "I'm going to work on my fort."

Granny said, "Do a good job, you hear? And make sure you shut the barn door when you go in. I don't want Sadie getting back out this afternoon. I don't want to have to find her."

I could hear Chesler mumbling. I knew he was talking about Sadie. He did not like Sadie, and Sadie did not like him.

The Christmas Portrait Surprise

Evie called to him. "Chesler, get your building done in a hurry, buddy. We won't be here long today. Granny has things to do, and we need to get back home."

I followed Evie and Granny inside and just stayed quiet. There were Christmas tins on the breakfast table, and I thought maybe Granny was sending cookies and fudge home with us. But then I heard her tell Evie that everybody was to bring Christmas treats for the road trip. She'd made the Christmas goodies for her friends. She wasn't thinking about us.

Granny Grace went to the refrigerator and pulled out an egg carton and what was left in the milk bottle. "Here, Evie, take these home. They'll just spoil before I get back."

"Thanks, but are you sure you don't want to give this to the Hortons?"

"No, she came up this morning, and I gave her a box of fruit and vegetables to take home, and a dozen eggs. Besides, Cecil will be getting the eggs every day."

Granny turned around and looked at me still standing at the breakfast table. "Kate, wait right there. I'll be back. I need to get something."

Evie came over and put the milk and eggs on the table. "Kate, I know you're not happy, but could you just try to be a little more understanding of Granny Grace and be sweet to her before she leaves? Nothing good will come of giving her the stink eye and the cold shoulder. You'll still feel bad, and she'll leave feeling worse. You're just punishing both of you."

"'Stink eye'? What does that mean? I never heard that before. I haven't even been looking at Granny. How could I give her the stink eye?"

"You're smart enough to figure out what 'stink eye' means. And whether or not you've been looking at Granny, I imagine she feels like you've been giving her the stink eye."

I felt Evie's hand on my shoulder, and she brushed my hair back. "Just try, Kate. For your sake and Granny's."

I looked at her, but I didn't say anything.

Granny Grace came back into the kitchen carrying a suit box tied with green Christmas ribbon. It looked like the box Mama used to put my Christmas dress in. She made me a new one every Christmas and wrapped it in the same box. Granny just stood there holding that box like she didn't know what to do with it. She finally said, "Katherine Joy, I need you to do something this Christmas. This is not just something you're doing for me. It's for the whole family."

I knew there was no Christmas dress in that box for me. Evie had already bought me one when she bought my bralettes.

"Will you do it?"

I didn't know what to say, and I really didn't want to say anything. But then I understood "stink eye" because I got it from Evie. "Yes, ma'am."

Granny Grace handed the box to me. "Now, Kate, this is your responsibility this year. This is our family Christmas tablecloth, and you know what to do with it. The cloth and several markers are in this box."

"But, Granny, this fits your dining table, the one Grandpa made. And we always sign the cloth on Christmas Eve after we eat French onion soup and grilled cheese sandwiches. You won't even be here. And what about Aunt Susannah Hope? She probably wants this tablecloth."

"That's right. I won't be here. But I've had a talk with your aunt, and she wants you to have this tablecloth as much as I do. So now it's yours, and it will go on the Harding Christmas table, onion-soup stains and all. Just make sure everyone signs it. You know this tablecloth has been in the family for over forty Christmases, but it's yours now. It's up to you to carry on this tradition as long as there's room on this cloth for our family to sign their names."

This time, I really didn't know what to say. My heart felt like it did the day Evie and Daddy got married, happy and sad all at the same time. "I'll do it, Granny, and thank you." I looked down at the box and back at Granny. Her eyes and mine were floating in tears. "I hope you have a good time on your trip." I held onto that box as tight as I could and put one arm out to hug Granny.

She hugged me back the way only Granny Grace can hug. "It'll be a fine Christmas, Kate. You just wait and see. A fine Christmas."

Granny followed us out the door, and Evie called to Chesler. He came running with Sadie right behind him.

Granny hollered, "Chesler, what did I tell you about the barn door? Now put your things down and go catch her."

Evie went to help him while I was putting the Christmas box in the car. Granny stood on the back steps and watched the chase. When they got Sadie in the barn, I heard Evie tell Chesler to ask Granny if something was okay and to kiss her bye. He put down his toolbox and hugged Granny good, and then we left.

I held the box in my lap all the way home. Chesler asked, "What you got, Kate?"

"The Christmas tablecloth. Granny gave it to me. You remember the one we all sign at Christmas?"

"I 'member. Look, Granny gave us some fudge and Christmas candy. And I got a special box too. Look. I found it in the barn, and Granny said I could have it. It's locked, and I can't get it open. But it's mine."

I looked at the old rusty metal box and wondered what was inside.

Chapter Nine

———————— ◆ ————————

Friday morning, December 20
Cedar Falls

Granny Grace

The farmhouse seemed especially quiet this morning, like it was as sad as I was that I was leaving. With just me here, the house had its own noises: the rhythm of the heater, the buzzing of lights, the creaking of the floor, the branches tapping against the windows. Even Sadie, who was better than a watchdog, was quiet. I'd not spent many nights away from this house since Joseph and I moved in years ago. Only a few nights when the family needed me—when Joseph was in the hospital, when John needed me with Diana Joy, and when Baby Hank was born and Susannah Hope needed me. Only when someone needed me. But now my family needed each other and to build their own Christmas traditions without me.

I checked the windows, doors, and the thermostat, and unplugged the coffee pot. The house was secure and silent. I heard John's truck in the driveway. He left it idling and came bustling through the back door. "Grace, you ready?"

I turned out the last light over the sink and felt like I

was turning out the Christmas lights for the last time before they went back into the attic. "As ready as I'm going to be. My bags are there next to the door." I grabbed my tote and the Christmas tins with my goodies and followed John to the truck. "It's a frosty morning. Colder's coming."

John put my bag in the front seat between us and draped the garment bag over it. "Yes, ma'am, it is, but my truck's warm, and yours will be too when you get back home." He put the truck in reverse, looked back through the rearview window, and backed out of the driveway.

"Sure do thank you for taking care of my truck and for picking me up so early. I guess Henrietta knows us old folks get up early and we might as well get on the road."

"You do have quite a drive according to Matt. About seven hours, he said when he came by last night. And I think we might have some snow and ice coming, so it's best if you're on your way before then."

I looked longingly at my front porch and my rocking chairs as we drove away. "Matt's a mighty fine pastor to drive us, especially during the Christmas season. That's a busy time for him. You sure married into a fine family when you married Evie. And I think Matt and his wife are mighty glad you got Evie to say yes. They get to see her now and feel better about her safety when she's not traveling the world."

"You're kind to say that, Grace, but I married into a fine O'Donnell family too. You truly took me in when I fell in love with Diana Joy. You became family to me and my brother Luke. You know, Luke told me I should take Diana's last name when we got married. That's how much like an O'Donnell we felt."

"We did become family, didn't we? I miss the way out of Diana Joy, and how I wish she was still with us. But she's not, and I know she would want you to find love again, and especially with someone who'd be a good parent to her children. God provided His answers in His due time for all of you. And now you're having your first Christmas as a family. Oh, I know Evie was part of our Christmas last year, but this is one is different."

I saw John wipe his cheek. "Yes, ma'am. It is. I'm so grateful that Evie is such an emotionally healthy person. She's not threatened by my love for Diana Joy, and she's understanding that Diana Joy is still a presence in our lives. Diana Joy was my whole world, and I was planning on growing old with her."

"Yes, she was your whole world, and you were hers until she went to heaven. Then your world changed. God had other plans—not that He gave Diana Joy cancer, but He looked out for you and the children when He brought Evie into your lives."

"Yes, and I'm grateful. Evie said she figured this family had enough love to go around, and if we could love her just a bit like we loved Diana Joy, she would be happy. We got enough love, Grace. Evie had a loving family growing up, but she's been a strong, single, independent woman for the last twenty years, so this whole family thing is almost new to her. She's still figuring things out, but she's patient with all of us."

"And you're patient with her. Seems like Chesler has really taken to her. She's good for him with that free spirit of hers, a little like Diana Joy's adventuresome spirit."

"Yep. She's the one who suggested I put his toolbox together for him. There was no waiting until Christmas either." John took a big swallow of the coffee from his insulated mug.

"Speaking of the toolbox, what was in that old metal box he took home yesterday? I didn't have time to even ask him where he found it. I just told him he could have it."

"Don't know what's in it yet. I had a couple of emergency calls last night, so the box is still out in the garage. We'll get to it. Said he found it digging in the back corner of the barn behind the horse stall."

"What was he digging for? I thought he was building his fort up in the loft."

"Guess I need to go see what that boy's been doing in your barn. Said he stacked up some old boards and bales of hay in the loft for his fort. But when I gave him that worn-out tarp and tent stakes and told him how he could make a tent, he figured out he couldn't put those stakes in that wooden floor of the loft. That wood's so old it's probably petrified. He needed dirt for the stakes to be secure, so I guess he's putting up his tent behind the horse stall. He probably found the box when he was digging to put his stakes in the ground."

"Since we don't have a horse or any barn animals except for the guineas, I've been thinking about pouring some concrete flooring in the barn."

"Unless you have water coming in there eroding the dirt, I'd leave it like it is. That packed dirt's probably been there more than a hundred years. Besides, it's not good to pour concrete next to those beams unless you leave two or three inches between the floor and the outside walls. Concrete holds moisture, and you'd be constantly replacing rotted beams. I'll take a look. If water's getting in and the dirt's eroding, then some fine pea gravel may be a better option. Don't worry about it, Grace. Luke and I will take care of whatever needs to be done."

"Then I'll check that one off my worry list. You boys do a fine job of taking care of me and this old farmstead. And just to remind you, the back part of that barn is original to the place and is probably a hundred and fifty years old. Joseph and I added on the front part and the horse stall and a place for his tractor. But he just couldn't bring himself to tear down the old barn and put a brand-new one in its place. He had a sense that some of his ancestors nailed those boards together, and he wanted them just as they were."

"I can see why. I'd imagine that old barn and shed on the back side could tell some stories." John pulled into the church parking lot and parked as close as he could to the church van.

The back doors of the van were open, and I saw Henrietta standing there with her clipboard. "Now, John, look around. You're the youngest man here, and that means you'll get stuck loading the luggage into the back of the van if you hang around. Don't you have somewhere to be in a hurry?" I winked at him.

He opened the truck door. "I'm happy to help, Grace. Matt will have the unloading to do on the other end. The least I can do is to help him get all that stuff onboard."

"Like I said, you're a good man, John." He helped me out of the truck and carried my bags to the van.

Henrietta was dressed like a Christmas elf in red stretch pants and top and a striped Christmas hat that looked like a candy cane. I suppose she had taken her own advice to dress comfortably for the drive. "Good morning, Grace. Where's all your luggage?" She handed me several tennis ball-sized red-green-and-white pompoms made out of yarn. "Lottie made these for us. Just tie them to your luggage handles. They'll help identify our bags in the hotel lobby."

"Thank you. John has my things. I have my tote bag and my tins of goodies." I saw five bright purple bags and a garment bag already decked out with the pompoms tied to the handles behind Henrietta. I took two pompoms from the wad she gave me and handed her the rest. "I just have the one garment bag and a suitcase. I don't need one on my tote bag. It's red, and I'll be carrying it with me all the time."

"One bag and a suitcase? How on earth did you get everything in that?"

"It wasn't a problem." I walked around behind her. "I suppose these six bags are yours." I saw Rose walking toward the van with her garment bag and rolling one suitcase. John rushed over to help her. "I guess it's a good thing Rose and I sacrificed so you could carry your six bags. That way we don't have to rent a trailer for yours."

"There's plenty of room, Grace. That's why I didn't set a bag limit. And besides, I have to carry extra things to make sure we have a fabulous trip."

"I'm sure it'll all be fine, Henrietta." I watched John load up the van as carefully as he would load up a patient in his ambulance, stacking and arranging every bag neatly and securely.

He came over and stood next to me when he finished. "I think that's all but Matt's bag. I see his car, but I don't see him. He's probably in his office doing some last-minute things. I think I'll say goodbye and head on to work." He hugged me and kissed my cheek. "Now, Grace, from what Evie told me, I know why you're really going on this trip. I don't think it's necessary, but apparently you do. So I will respect your wishes, and I do hope you'll have a good time. We will miss you like crazy, but we'll do our celebrating when you get home. Love you, and behave, okay?" John smiled and walked away.

I didn't need to say a word. Instead, I stood quietly alone while the others approached the van. Then I felt Henrietta's arm around me. "Come on, Grace, you're sitting with me. I might not have been the smartest girl in my class, but I'm smart enough to know you have some of that fudge with the peppermint bark topping in one of those Christmas tins. And you'll be glad to know I brought two pillows with silk pillowcases so our hair won't get messed up, and I'll share my blanket with you too. We're going to have a fabulous time."

We made our way to the van. When everyone else was seated, she told me to take the window seat and that she needed to get something from a bag in the back. I had no idea how she would find what she needed, but Matt was there now to help her.

Carl had taken a seat in the back with Lottie and Rose. Roger was riding shotgun as the pilot. I took my seat in the front row behind the driver and next to the window. When Henrietta returned with a brown paper bag, Matt helped her up the step and closed the door. She sat down beside me.

As soon as Matt got in and cranked up, Henrietta started pulling something out of the bag and shouting as though we wouldn't be able to hear her. "Don't put it in Drive yet, Matt. As the leader of this trip, I'm always prepared, and here are the barf bags in case anyone gets sick." She started passing them out. "We can always stop if you need some air and to walk around. And if anyone needs first aid, I have a first-aid kit in the back. We're going to have a fabulous time. Now, I've asked Matt to pray for us."

That was three times this morning Henrietta has told us we were going to have a fabulous time. Who was she trying to convince? Maybe me, and I thought I could use some convincing. And now she was passing out barf bags and asking the pastor to pray? A fabulous time?

Matt obliged. "Dear Father, thank You for hearing our prayers this morning. We are grateful that we're all here together on the edge of an adventure. We are the blessed of the blessed to be able to take a trip like this when so many in the world are just struggling to live. We're almost embarrassed to ask You for anything else, Father, but we ask for Your protection as we travel, and that in Your mercy, You would keep us all safe and healthy. We're leaving behind some folks we love, and we ask that You take care of them while we are apart, especially with the weather coming in. And Lord, help us to always remember the real meaning of Christmas. Remind us to practice grace, mercy, and kindness with each other, and help us reflect Your light every place we stop along the way. Amen."

Everyone echoed his amen. Matt turned on the Christmas music, and we were off. Henrietta was shuffling papers and returning them to her green folder. Lottie was knitting and chattering away in the back, explaining to Rose how she and her granddaughter made the pompoms for our luggage. I didn't turn to see, but I figured Carl's eyes were rolling, if they were even open. Carl could outdo me with his eyerolling. Roger was studying a map, and Matt was tapping his finger on the steering wheel in rhythm to "Joy to the World," probably wondering what he'd gotten himself into but happy nonetheless. I was quietly pondering the same thing, enjoying the carols, and asking God more specifically to take care of Katherine Joy's heart. I wanted there to be joy in her world.

Chapter Ten

---◆---

Saturday morning, December 21
Cedar Falls

Kate

I was shivering. The snow was beginning to come down, and the wind was blowing hard. I held tight to the grocery cart. Evie was going through her bag again trying to find her car keys. "Do you need me to help?"

"Thanks, Kate. I know they're in here. There's just nowhere to dump all this mess out. I think I need a smaller bag."

At least the groceries wouldn't spoil out here if it took her a while, but they might freeze. *And me too.* I pulled up the hood of my coat and marched in place at the car trunk, trying to stay warm.

Evie shouted above the wind. "I found them." She unlocked the trunk, and we loaded it with a week's worth of groceries. I'd made sure she got extra of everything.

With the last bag in, she said, "Hop in and let's go."

"But I have to return the grocery cart. Mama always said that was the responsible thing to do."

"Of course you must. Sorry. I think this cold wind has

rattled my brain." She got in the car and cranked up then followed me slowly to the front of the grocery store.

I pushed the cart and mumbled under my breath. "Your brain stays rattled. It would be so much easier if you'd just put the keys in the same place in your bag every time. And when you get home, hang them on the key rack Daddy made and hung at the door. You're always wasting time and making the rest of us kill time while we wait on you to find your keys. Late to school. Late to church. Granny Grace says it's a sin to waste time. She's says if you're going to kill time, you should work it to death. I'll probably die and go to hell for sinning with my angry thoughts while you're looking for your blooming car keys."

I returned the cart and hopped into the car. Evie looked at me curiously. "Kate, were you talking to yourself?"

"I guess I was. Just complaining about how cold it is."

"Well, you might as well keep complaining, because the weather forecast says more cold and high winds are on the way. Complaining always helps, you know." Evie turned toward me and grinned. "Maybe we'll even have a white Christmas. At least we got all the groceries we need, so we should be good for a few days."

I knew Evie was trying, and I knew she was right about complaining. But my complaining had worked a little. She did ask me to help her make the grocery list last night so that we'd have everything we needed for the next few days with Christmas coming. I got three gallons of milk—enough for breakfast and to make pancakes and lots of hot chocolate. She didn't fuss about it.

"I was wondering. The Christmas shopping is done, and the grocery shopping. And I know Laramie and her family are leaving for Virginia today. So I was thinking if you don't have anything to do this afternoon, you might help me in the darkroom. I need to finish up one job for a client, and then I'll be done with my work until after New Year's. Do you have something else you want to do, or could you help me?"

"Sure. I can help." I liked working in the darkroom. She was teaching me how to develop my own pictures.

"Perfect. If I can get these in the frames today, I can deliver them to Mrs. Muldoon at church tomorrow. Last minute, she wanted some photos of her grandchildren dressed up for Christmas. I think she's planning a surprise for her daughter. Your handwriting is so much better for the labels."

"Thank you. I'll be happy to help. I don't have anything else to do. I'd thought about calling Aunt Susannah Hope to see if she needs me to babysit this afternoon."

"I'm sure she'd appreciate the offer, and if you'd rather do that . . ." Evie mashed the button to open the garage door.

"Not really. I'd rather work in the darkroom."

"I like having you around and working with me. But you can't be snooping around in there. It is Christmas after all, and I still have a few Christmas surprises for the family."

"I can keep a secret, you know. Just don't ever tell Chesler something you don't want everybody to know. That boy cannot keep a secret, unless it's his own and he knows if he tells he's gonna be in trouble."

"Thanks for the warning, but I already figured that one out after he told your daddy what we had for his birthday." She turned the car off and dropped her keys in her bag.

"Oops, why don't you put your keys on the rack next to the door? The one Daddy made for you."

"Good idea. Thanks for reminding me." She got her keys out of the bag and put them in her jacket pocket. "Let's get these groceries put away and make some lunch. Your daddy and Chesler should be back by then. They went out to Granny Grace's to batten down the hatches with the storm coming in, and John was wanting to see what Chesler's been doing in the barn."

It took us four trips to get all the groceries inside. We hung up our jackets in the mudroom, and I got the keys out of Evie's jacket pocket and hung them on the rack next to the door. At least I would know where they were when we needed them.

When we started putting the groceries away, Evie asked, "Now what was it about the ground beef and sausage? In the freezer or not?"

I was putting the canned goods in the pantry. "Not. When the weather is cold, Daddy always makes chili when Uncle Luke comes over. Remember, he and Aunt Lisa are coming over tomorrow night."

"I remember. Lisa's bringing the twice-baked potatoes."

Uncle Luke had always stayed with us for the holidays until he married Aunt Lisa. That was another change at Christmas. But he was finished with medical school, and they'd moved back from Boston. They had their own house now.

"Does your daddy make good chili? He's never made it for us."

"It's real good. That's just about all Daddy knew how to cook when he was raising Uncle Luke after their parents died in that wreck. Uncle Luke won't eat anybody's chili except for Daddy's. He thinks it's the best."

Evie folded up the last paper bag and put it in the pantry. "Then I'll really look forward to that. I think it's fantastic that your daddy is finishing his training as a physician's assistant and will be working with your Uncle Luke by next summer. I don't think I've ever seen any brothers as close as those two are. I guess the hard times they went through together made them really depend on each other."

"Probably it did." I didn't want to talk any more about hard times and sticking together. I went to the sink to wash my hands. The redbird was perched in the juniper tree again. That bird always knew when to show up. She sat there all perky, looking at me, cocking her head one way and then the other, like she was asking me why I wasn't being nicer to Evie. I could have asked her why she didn't help me keep Granny Grace at home for Christmas.

———•———

Saturday morning
Old Edwards Inn, Highlands, NC

Granny Grace

I was ready for my cup of coffee. It was nearly nine o'clock, and I usually had my first cup before sunup. We were so worn out from the drive yesterday that we didn't take time to do anything but check in, have dinner, and go to bed. Henrietta had set breakfast for nine o'clock and reserved us a table. We went downstairs early so she could check on things.

While she spoke with someone in the dining room, I walked around the lobby. Historic elegance but so comfortable and inviting. Far better than the brochures. What I saw was like the front page of a travel magazine and a history book combined. But it smelled and sounded like Christmas. Couldn't get that from a photo. The fragrance of fresh green wreaths on the windows, the live Christmas trees twinkling, the fire crackling, and I thought I got a waft of hot cider. And somewhere a harp was playing "I Wonder as I Wander." Rather appropriate for me this morning, wondering what on earth I was doing here wandering around such a beautiful place at Christmas.

I felt Henrietta's tug. "Oh, this place is something, isn't it, Grace? Just look. It's nothing short of magical. Wouldn't you agree?"

"I would. 'Magical' is a good word." *Magic. Oh, if I could have waved my wand and been back in my farmhouse in Cedar Falls.* "I think I'd be better company if I had a cup of coffee."

"Well, just follow me. Everybody's already seated at the table, and the waiter is bringing a whole fresh pot just for us. That's some kind of service we're getting." She led me into the dining room. "Look, Roger saved you this seat so you could look out the window. Why it looks like a Christmas card out there with that blanket of snow on those mountains in the distance."

I sat down and put my red bag under my chair. "Yes, and this place is something else. I expect Charles Dickens himself to come through the door any minute."

Henrietta sat down on the other side of the table and spoke to everyone. "Now, eat yourself a hearty breakfast, because we'll be out most of the day seeing the town. You're on your own for a light lunch as we walk Main Street, and then we'll have a lovely dinner right here this evening. It's going to be a fabulous day today, snow and all."

I looked at Roger. "What sounds good for breakfast besides a cup of coffee?"

"Well, Grace, I've already looked over the menu, and it reads like a southern novel—a lot of delicious detail. And it all sounds good, but I'll be having my regular breakfast—black coffee, oatmeal with berries, and a slice of dry toast. So what looks good to you?"

"Anything but that. I'm here, and I probably won't pass this way again, so I'm going to have myself a special breakfast. The grits bowl with diced country ham, pimento cheese, and a fried egg on top with a splash of red-eye gravy sounds good to me. And I do believe they have biscuits. Probably not as good as Lottie's, but I'll know after I eat one."

"Atta girl, Grace! Enjoy yourself," Roger replied.

Lottie got up from her chair and went for the coffee pot at the end of the table. Henrietta stopped her. "Lottie, put yourself right back in your chair. I know you're the consummate host back in Cedar Falls, and you don't like the looks of empty coffee cups, but you're on vacation."

A young man dressed in black trousers, white shirt, and red bow tie was at Lottie's side like a flash. "Ma'am, allow me to serve you and your breakfast companions. This is fresh coffee made with freshly ground coffee beans from Ethiopia—the best coffee in the world."

Carl spoke for the first time. "Did everybody rest well last night? Sounds like we'll be out and about most of the day. Lottie, you put on your brakes mighty fast. You wearing your snow tires this morning?" Carl had a dry, sometimes wry sense of humor.

"No, Carl. I can stop on a dime, but I'll be hanging on to you this morning in case the sidewalks are slippery."

"I suppose everybody needs somebody else to hang on to." He turned to Roger. "Roger, we both have two arms and we have four fine ladies. Guess we'll all have somebody to hang on to today."

Carl was right. We did need someone to hang on to, and if I couldn't be with my family and hang onto them this Christmas, these folks were a mighty fine bunch to substitute. I turned to Rose. "You feeling okay, Rose? You're awfully quiet."

"I'm feeling very well, thank you, Grace. I'm just taking it all in, and I was just remembering what I read about the history of this property."

Henrietta interrupted, "Rose, would you tell us about it? I love the way you talk about history."

Rose lifted her chin and addressed us like we were students in her history class. "The Old Edwards Inn has quite a rich history, and it has always been known for its hospitality. The town of Highlands was founded post-Civil War in 1875 by developers who thought this a magnificent location, the crossroads of travel routes from New York City down to New Orleans and from Chicago to Savannah. Apparently the developers were right. Three years later, a gentleman built the two-and-a-half-story Central Inn, which became a boarding house."

Roger interrupted. "I guess this inn has seen its share of weary travelers."

Rose continued. "I suppose you're right about that. The inn's ownership has changed hands as people died and came and went. And of course it has been refurbished and added on to. But for the last hundred and twenty-five years, it's been known for its hospitality. I'm planning to ask the concierge to give me a quick tour this afternoon, and I'll be able to give you more detail at dinner."

Carl answered, "I think I'd like to take that tour with you, Rose. I've always been a bit of a history buff myself, albeit I'm more interested in old farm implements. Farm machinery can tell us acres about the development of this country."

Rose smiled gently. "I never thought of it that way, Carl. But you are certainly right. From commerce to the table, it tells a story."

Henrietta blurted out, "So much for the past. Now Roger, if you were at home this morning, just what would you be doing?"

Roger put down his coffee cup. "Well, to start with, I wouldn't be at home. This Saturday before Christmas will be a busy day at the bank—folks getting that last-minute cash to do their shopping. I imagine I'd be hanging around the bank lobby handing out candy canes and wishing our good customers a Merry Christmas. Important work, you know. People like feeling appreciated. Yes, they do."

Henrietta said, "That would certainly put you in the Christmas spirit. I went to the bank's little soiree you had last week. Bringing in that grand piano from Lexington and that fine pianist was a great idea and a gift to the community. I think they'll be having music here tonight. My, we have so much to look forward to today, out walking Main Street, in and out of shops. I know that will put us in the Christmas spirit. And then they're having cookie decorating for the children this afternoon." She giggled. "Carl, I know you and Roger would enjoy that. They might even have an apron to fit you."

She looked at Lottie. "And Lottie B, what would you be doing if you were at home instead of off with this fun group in such a fabulous place?"

"From what I saw on the weather report this morning, with a winter storm headed our way, I'd be stoking the fire and knitting my snowflake afghan. Sounds like I might need it."

Carl chuckled. "Lottie, I have sore ribs this morning from your constant jabbing me all day yesterday with your elbow or your knitting needles. I think you need to sit in the pilot's seat on the way home. You're dangerous. The only time you didn't have those knitting needles in your hand was when you were nibbling on some of Grace's fudge. I didn't know anybody could knit for eight hours straight." Carl surveyed the room. "And by the way, where's Matt this morning?"

Roger answered, "He called his wife last night and listened to the weather report. He decided to get an early start to get home before the storm. We went to get his rental car last night, and he left at five o'clock this morning. That'll put him home early afternoon, well before the storm comes in."

Henrietta continued her rollcall question. "Rose, what would you be doing if you were back home in Cedar Falls?"

Rose lifted her chin again and sighed long. "Well, I volunteer at the library on Saturdays, and for the past several years, I've had a Christmas-story reading time with the children on the Saturday afternoon before Christmas. Dan picks up my antique maple Windsor rocking chair, delivers it to the library, and places it next to the tree. The children bring their pillows and blankets and sit around me on the floor, and I read stories all afternoon. They come and go, but they're quiet and respectful, and I entertain them by using my quirky voices. Only an old lady like me could get by with that."

"Rose, you're so well-loved in Cedar Falls, I imagine you could get by with anything. My grandson Chesler will miss you today. He and Kate have been hearing your stories for the last few years. Kate probably thinks she's too old for that anymore."

Rose's gentle smile appeared. "I recall your sweet grandchildren. Kate brought the quilt you and your daughters made for her, the one with the embroidered redbird in the middle. She took good care of her little brother and kept him still and quiet. I have images of them huddled together like two little birds themselves, wrapped in that quilt. And I remember Kate would mouth the words of some of the stories as though she had them memorized."

My chin quivered and my eyes swam with tears, and I didn't wait for Henrietta's probing question. "Yes, like two little birds. I'd have my arms wrapped around those two little birds if I were home this morning." Movement out the window caught my eye. A scarlet redbird, perched on the snow-flocked pine branches and shining in the morning sun.

Chapter Eleven

---◆---

Saturday afternoon, December 21
Cedar Falls

Kate

"Kate, you are such good help in the darkroom. I wouldn't even be close to finished if you hadn't helped me." Evie backed away from the table and looked at the framed photographs. "Do you think Mrs. Muldoon will be happy with these?"

"She will. Most grannies really like pictures of their grandchildren." I couldn't help but wondering what Granny Grace was doing right now. "She might want them this afternoon." I hoped Evie would take me up on the delivery nudge so I could be alone for a while.

"I was planning to see her at church tomorrow and deliver them, but that's not a bad idea. I think I'll give her a call. Would you like to go with me?" Evie started wrapping the frames in brown paper.

"I don't think so. I have something I need to do here." I was walking toward the door when Chesler let out one of his paint-peeling screams. "Good grits, that boy has lungs. I'll go check on him."

The Christmas Portrait Surprise

"Do I hear your dad too?"

I was out the door and down the hall. "Yes, ma'am. They're both hollering. I'll see what happened." I ran to the garage and opened the door. Daddy and Chesler were standing wide eyed, staring at the metal box on Daddy's workbench. "Is there blood anywhere?"

Chesler was jumping up and down by then. "I'm not bleeding. But look, Kate. It's treasure, and it's mine."

I walked over to the workbench and watched Daddy lift out a bundle of rotted old fabric from the metal box. "What is that?"

"Well, I'm not sure. I finally got it opened. Looks like an old quilt, but there's something else here." Daddy laid the bundle on his workbench and started unwrapping. "Whoever buried this buried it a long time ago. It is an old quilt with something else here." The threads were coming apart in Daddy's hands. "Yep, another box."

Chesler had his nose right in it. "Does it have a lock?"

Daddy turned the smaller box over in his hands. "No. No lock. Just rust like the other one, but not quite as much. Hand me that flathead screwdriver, please."

Chesler handed it to him. "Hurry, Daddy. It's got to be treasure. Buried treasure. It's mine 'cause I found it."

Daddy was as careful as he was when he stitched up Chesler's leg. He worked the screwdriver under the rim of the lid and inched it along the front of the box and down each side. "Ah, here it comes." He opened it and lifted out another small bundle. "Now this looks like old wool."

Chesler was leaning over the workbench, his feet not even reaching the floor. "Unfold it, Daddy. Hurry. I want to see. It's a treasure. I know it is."

"I doubt it's a treasure, son. Just hold your horses. It's not going anywhere, and whatever it is has been in these two boxes a long time." Daddy kept unfolding.

And then, there it was. Chesler's eyes were as big as his open mouth, and so were Daddy's.

About that time Evie walked into the garage. "What's all this commotion going on out here?"

Daddy held several coins in his hand. "Well, I'm not sure, but I think Chesler has dug up an old treasure in Granny's barn."

"See, I told you. It's mine, and I'm going back to dig some more."

Evie stepped closer and almost whispered. "John, that looks like gold."

Daddy said, "Um-huh. That's what I thought it was."

She put her hand on Chesler's head and turned him to look at her. "And Chesler, this is what you dug up in Granny's barn?"

"Yes ma'am. I dug it up when I was putting up my tent in the back of the barn. It's mine. Granny said I could have it."

I knew where this conversation was headed, like two trains colliding on a railroad track. Daddy spoke up, "Well, son, we'll have to see what Granny says about this when she gets home. After all, you did find it on her property."

Granny. Home. I got an idea. "We should call her. This looks really valuable and important. I think she would want to see it before Christmas. Maybe it belonged to someone in Grandpa's family."

Daddy said, "That farm has been in the O'Donnell family for generations, so you're probably right. But we may never know how this got there."

Evie picked up a coin. "I'm headed to call Matt."

Daddy asked, "Why do you need to call your brother? He might not even be home yet. And besides, if he is, he's probably preparing his sermon for tomorrow."

"Matt has been a coin collector since he was a child.

He'd be a good place to start to see what these are." Evie put the coin back on the wool covering.

Daddy turned the coin over and wiped it on his shirt sleeve. "It's hard to see the imprint. They're a bit tarnished." "All the more reason to ask Matt. I tell you, he knows about these things."

I wasn't about to miss my opportunity. "Yes, and we should call Granny. She might know something. Maybe she forgot the box was there."

Daddy put the coins back in the cloth and into the box. "Guess we should put these in a safe place until we can talk to Matt." Then Daddy looked at me. "And we'll tell Granny Grace all about this when she gets home. It will be like an added Christmas surprise. Other than asking Matt about the coins, I think we should keep them a secret. If somebody thinks there's buried treasure in Granny's barn, the barn might be torn down and the ground might be plowed up by treasure hunters by the time Granny gets back."

I could only hope that Granny would call that night. And if she did, she was going to hear all about the treasure Chesler had dug up in the barn. No way Chesler could keep quiet about that for almost a week, even if it did mean the barn would be torn down.

Evie left to deliver Mrs. Muldoon's photographs. Chesler had gone off to play, and Daddy was reading something on his computer screen. I grabbed my coat and gloves. "I'm going down by the creek. I'll be back in a few minutes."

Daddy looked up. "Wait a minute. It's cold out there. Why are you going to the creek?"

"I need to cut some branches before the storm comes in tomorrow night."

"You need some help? I can go with you and make short order of it."

"No, sir. I'll be fine. You stay with Chesler and keep the

fire going. And you really should start on the chili. Remember Uncle Luke and Aunt Lisa are coming tomorrow night, and chili's always better the second day."

"Thanks for the reminder." He turned back to his computer screen.

I got the clippers and a bucket from the garage and headed out back toward the creek. The sky was gray, but the wind wasn't so bad. None of the little pools near the creek bank had frozen yet, but by this time tomorrow afternoon, they would probably be ice.

A redbird was perched in the fir tree at the edge of the forest. She chirped, and I tried to answer. I wished I could learn to make bird sounds. Grandpa could. He could call a turkey a half a mile away.

I walked closer. The bird flew deeper into the forest, and I followed her. I knew I'd find the holly tree and pine I wanted if I went into the woods.

I was clipping some pine branches when I heard Daddy whistling "I Wonder as I Wander." He was a good whistler, and he could play the harmonica. He used to play it for Mama when they would sit on the front porch after supper in the summertime. Then, when she got really sick, he didn't play it or whistle anymore. He did now that Evie's around.

I didn't even turn around to see. "Why don't you whistle 'Jingle Bells,' Daddy? It's a happier tune."

There was no answer. I called out again. "Daddy?"

A faintly familiar voice answered, "Well, hello, there, Katherine Joy. Haven't seen you in a while."

I turned quickly. I knew it was Mister Josh. And there he was. Same old coat and hood with his long gray hair poking out. And that same scruffy gray beard and bushy eyebrows and little sky-blue eyes. Just like he was when I got locked in the church overnight on Christmas Eve. He had been there when I was so scared and couldn't get out to get back home. Said he needed someplace warm to spend the night. Chesler had been in on my secret plan to take Mama's Christmas present to the church after the Christmas Eve services. I had decided that getting her present to the church was my only chance of getting it to Mama in heaven. My plan hadn't included getting locked in the church, but I had been glad Mister Josh showed up. He talked to me about Mama, but he had disappeared before Daddy and Uncle Luke found me on Christmas morning. And Mama's gift had disappeared with him.

Nobody had believed my story, but I had found Mister Josh's matches in my coat pocket—the matches He used to light the Christ candle so we could see that night. I had seen Mister Josh a couple of times since that Christmas, and he hadn't changed. "Mister Josh. I thought you were my daddy. He whistles too. You're back?"

I heard his soft chuckle. He stepped closer. "Back from where, little one?"

"I don't know. You just haven't been around. I haven't seen you in a while, and I've been looking. I thought maybe you'd never come back, and I wouldn't see you ever again."

"Oh, I'm always around. I don't venture too far." He pulled down the holly limb for me to reach it. "Last time I saw you here, you were out picking flowers to make a nosegay for your aunt Susannah Hope. How's she doing?"

"She's doing good, and so is little Hank."

"And how about Cecil and Sugar?"

I put the branch in the bucket. "They're doing good too. And Mrs. Horton had another baby. Granny Grace and the church ladies helped them a lot. And Cecil's daddy has a good job driving a truck now."

"Glad to hear that. Everybody needs a little help now and then." He reached down in the bucket.

I stopped clipping branches and looked up at him. "You must really be real if you remember about my aunt and Cecil and Sugar."

"Now tell me what makes you think I'm not really real."

"Because nobody believes me when I tell them about you. And nobody else sees you. Daddy says that you're just my imagination. I have a good imagination, but it's not that good. And you gave me the matches that Christmas Eve when I got locked in the church and it was dark. So you're not my imagination."

"No. I'd say I'm pretty real. You heard me whistle, and we're having this conversation. I'm no more your imagination than you are my imagination, Kate. So, tell me what you're planning to do with the holly and pine. More nosegays?"

"Kinda. I'm making Christmas sprigs for Evie and my two aunts. Storm's coming tomorrow, so I figured I'd better get down here before the ice and snow get here."

"That's a mighty thoughtful present." He sat down on the log next to the holly tree.

"Oh, it's not a present. I made their presents. The Christmas sprig goes in the ribbon on the package."

"Now, you told me before about the meaning of the blossoms you put in the nosegay for your aunt and how your mama had taught you about the meaning of flowers. Any meaning to what you have in the bucket?"

I put my bucket down and reached in and pulled out some branches. "Mama taught me that holly means happiness, and pine means peace." I picked up a sprig of juniper with blue berries. "Juniper is a symbol of protection. Did you know that bugs and worms don't bother juniper trees?"

"So glad you told me that."

"Mama said juniper also means forever. You know, like

eternity. And that's what the fir means too. That's why we have fir Christmas trees. Mama said because of Christmas we have forever. So every Christmas we had to have a fir for our Christmas tree."

"Your mama was such a wise woman." He rubbed his beard. "I guess that's why the redbird liked to perch in the juniper trees, all protected forever."

"Maybe, but the birds like the juniper berries too." I had never really thought about why the redbird like the juniper trees. After what Mister Josh said, I knew I'd be thinking about Mama in heaven when I saw the bird in the juniper tree.

I sat down next to him and pulled a berry from the limb and squished it between my fingers until I found the seed. I handed the seed to him. "You see the seed. Mama said Indians used to make necklaces from them. We made a bracelet one time. She let me paint the seeds any color I wanted, and I painted them all different colors."

He took the seed and looked at it. "Amazing, this little seed." He took off his gloves and rolled the seed around in his hand. "Given enough time, Katherine Joy, this seed has a whole forest inside it." He pulled off his knitted cap and laid it on top of his old ratty gloves and ran his fingers through his hair. He needed some new gloves, but his hands looked strong and clean. "Looks like you're giving gifts of happiness, peace, protection, and eternity, and it sounds like you'll be having a fine and merry Christmas." He paused, but I didn't say a word. "I don't recall hearing you mention your Granny Grace."

I didn't know what to say, so I stayed quiet. So did he. He dropped the juniper seed to the ground and used his foot to cover it with leaves. Finally I said, "She's not here."

"I'm just supposing that doesn't make you very happy about Christmas." He turned to look at me. His face was all leathery and wrinkled. The whites of his eyes were whiter than fresh snow, and his small blue eyes were bluer than the sky on a summer day.

"Nope. I don't like Christmas so much anymore. Seems like every Christmas someone goes away. First Grandpa went to heaven, then Mama, and now Granny decided to take a trip. So she's off in North Carolina with some of her friends. Just left her family for Christmas. I begged her not to go, but she went anyway."

"I'm certain if your Granny decided to make a trip at Christmas, she had a good reason."

"She said she did, but I think we might get her to come home, though. My brother . . ." I remembered I wasn't supposed to tell anyone about the treasure Chesler found. Then I had an idea. This way everybody would know Mister Josh was real. I changed my tune and used my best manners Mama had taught me.

"Mister Josh, I would like to invite you to our house for Christmas. My whole family, except for Granny Grace, will be there. And Aunt Susannah Hope is a really good cook, and I'll be helping her. I think you'd like to come to our house. We have homemade cinnamon rolls with hot chocolate for breakfast, and then we open our presents and read the Christmas story. You can learn about Jesus. That's our tradition. Then we have the biggest lunch ever with the Christmas tablecloth on the table. You won't believe all the food we have with turkey and dressing and sweet potatoes and green beans and a red velvet cake for dessert. So much food I can't even remember it all. And you could sign the tablecloth just like everybody in our family. You could come, and you wouldn't have to bring any presents or anything." I looked again at his ratty old sweater. "And if you don't have a Christmas sweater, my daddy has one you could wear. It will be great, and then with you there, we wouldn't miss Granny Grace so much."

I don't think he even blinked his eyes the whole time I was saying all that. "Well, Katherine Joy, that's about the finest invitation I've ever had, and I thank you."

"You're welcome. I just figured you might need a family to be with at Christmas, and you could be our special guest. It would make my family so happy."

"You're right about needing a family to be with at Christmas. And I'm sure you'd be a mighty fine family to celebrate with, but I have lots of places to be and lots of people I need to see for Christmas."

"Oh." I was puzzled. He still looked like a homeless person.

"I think you'll have a happy time together with your family. And who knows? Christmas might even come with a surprise or two." He put his gloves and hood back on and stood up.

I lowered my voice. "I just thought you might be alone, and no one should be alone at Christmas."

"I think that's what Christmas is all about, don't you? No one has to be alone, ever. You listen good to the Christmas story, and you remember that, Katherine Joy."

I heard the redbird chirping and stood to look behind me. She was there, perched in the juniper tree. When I turned back around, Mister Josh was gone.

I called to him. "Mister Josh?" I looked all around me in the forest. "Mister Josh?" No answer, only the chirp of the redbird.

He was gone, but I could hear him. Somewhere in the tree branches, I could hear him whistling "I Wonder as I Wander."

Chapter Twelve

———————◆———————

Sunday morning, December 22
Old Edwards Inn

Granny Grace

My bags were packed, and I was dressed comfortably for the drive to Lexington. Henrietta was still getting ready. I knew Chesler would be singing his little heart out in church this morning, so I decided to call.

I picked up the hotel phone and dialed the number. John answered. "Good morning, John. I imagine you're getting ready for church. Or are you working today?"

John was chipper. "Ready for church and a relaxing afternoon by the fire. I'm on call if they need me. And I wouldn't be surprised if they do with the weather headed our way tonight. How are you making it on the trip?"

I twirled the phone cord around my finger. "Well, Henrietta keeps reminding me we're having a fabulous time, and I suppose we are. The Old Edwards Inn is the perfect picture of Christmas you see on the finest Christmas cards, and we've had such good food and beautiful music. We'll be heading out in a couple of hours for the drive to Lexington. Should be there middle of the afternoon. We'll miss Matt, but I think Roger will get us there safely. Did Matt get home okay?"

"I'm assuming he did or we would have heard. I'll be calling him this afternoon if I don't get to speak with him at church." There was a hesitancy in John's voice. "Grace, you know the metal box Chesler dug up in your barn?"

"That old rusty thing he found when he was building his fort?"

"Yes. You know anything about that box?"

"Not a thing. Never knew it was there until Chesler found it. Why? What about it?"

"I wasn't planning to tell you until you got home, but I changed my mind. I doubt Chesler can keep the news anyway. So it's best if you hear it straight from me."

"Now you have my attention. Something wrong? What was in the box?"

"Certainly nothing wrong. There were some old gold coins and a few pieces of silver flatware in the box. I mean, really old coins."

"Now that beats pigs flying! I can just imagine Chesler's excitement. I can tell you neither Joseph nor I buried the box."

"Wait, Grace. Can anyone hear you right now?"

I was puzzled. "No, I'm still in my room. Why do you ask me that?"

"Just think it best if we keep this to ourselves for right now. I know you're with friends you trust, but we just don't need this news getting out until we get more information."

"Okay. I'll keep this to myself. All I know is that the farm has been in Joseph's family since the days of his great grandparents back in the early eighteen hundreds. Seems I remember they sold off part of the land after the Great Depression, but there's still nearly three hundred acres, including the old family cemetery. But you already know all that, John. You've seen the cemetery."

"Yes, I have, but it's been a while. When you get home, maybe you and I need to go back to the cemetery and look around."

"Sure, after the snow melts. I would imagine whoever buried it was an ancestor. That part of the barn has been there a long time, and Joseph didn't know how long. He just knew he couldn't tear it down. Remember, you and I were just talking about the barn the other day."

"Yes, we were. We're keeping all this quiet, but with your permission, I'm planning to tell Matt. Evie told me he is a coin collector, and he might be helpful in getting the coins cleaned and assessed."

"Sure, John. I trust you with everything I have." I could hear Chesler in the background. "I hear Chesler. I promised to call him, so if you're done talking, I'd like to speak to him. I want to make sure he knows I haven't made it to the Indian burial ground."

John chuckled. "Certainly. You have a safe trip to Lexington, and let us hear from you, and remember not to tell anybody about the cache."

Chesler squealed as soon as he got the phone. "Hey, Granny. You gotta come home. There's a big surprise. You got to, Granny, 'cause Daddy said not to tell you until you get home."

"I'll be home on Friday, Chesler, just like I promised. You singing at church today?"

"Yes, ma'am. I'm singing a solo."

"Oh, I wish I could hear you, but I know you'll sing like an angel just like last year." That red-haired little fellow was tugging on my heart strings this morning. "Is Kate where I could speak with her?"

"Just a minute, Granny." Chesler hollered for Kate. "She's coming down the stairs."

The Christmas Portrait Surprise

Kate's voice was not so chipper. "Hi, Granny." Then silence.

"Good Sunday morning to you, Kate. Got on that beautiful green-velvet dress Evie bought for you?"

"Yes, ma'am." More silence.

I chuckled. "And the bralette?" Nothing. "I just wanted to check in. We're having a nice time, and we'll be driving back to Lexington today. I don't take pictures like you and Evie, but I can't wait for you to see my postcards. Maybe you and I can make a trip over here sometime. I think you'd like it."

Kate said so matter-of-factly, "Yes, ma'am. Mister Josh might be coming to our house for Christmas. I invited him."

I was always perplexed when Kate talked about Mister Josh. I wanted to believe her, but it made no sense. "So, you must have seen him again, then."

"I did. Yesterday, in the woods."

"In the woods again?"

"Yes, ma'am. I was cutting holly and pine and fir for Christmas sprigs. He was taking a walk. But anyway, I'm not sure if he's coming. I'm sorry you won't get to meet him if he does."

My heart sputtered a bit at the thought of Kate in the woods with this mysterious Mister Josh … if he was real. "I'm hoping you'll have a sweet Christmas whether Mister Josh comes or not. I'll be talking to you before then. Can you put your daddy back on the phone, please?"

Silence. The next voice I heard was John's. "John, first you tell me about a buried cache in the barn, and now Kate tells me she's invited Mister Josh for Christmas. What's going on with that?"

"First I heard of it. I'll ask her about it."

"She said she saw him again in the woods yesterday. I

don't too much like to think about that. Maybe she's just making it up to get my goat. And it worked. All right, I need to go. I'll check back with you when we get to Lexington and settled."

"Okay. Hope you have a safe drive today. It's best to get to where you're going before dark. And don't worry about your place. Chesler and I took a ride out yesterday and secured everything before the storm blows in."

"Thanks, John. Give my love to Evie. Bye for now." I hung up the phone and just sat on the bed for a minute to get my bearings. All these surprises, and I couldn't tell anyone. Not about what Chesler found, and I would not dare mention Mister Josh to my friends.

I walked to the door of the bathroom. Henrietta was standing in front of the mirror putting on another coat of red lipstick. I had politely refused when she offered the tube to me earlier. "Henrietta, more lipstick? We're going to be drinking cold coffee and missing breakfast, but don't worry about it, you'll have the reddest lips in Highlands."

"Oh, hush, Grace. You know how I am about my lipstick."

She followed me as I grabbed my tote bag from the bed and walked toward the door pulling my suitcase. "I do—all ten tubes of red. I didn't know red had so many shades."

She turned around and winked at me and straightened her scarf. "And Grace, I want you to promise to get all the girls to wear red lipstick for my funeral, and for once in your life, you have to wear it too."

"If promising to wear lipstick gets me out of this room, then I promise to wear all ten shades."

"Thank you, Grace. I may sit straight up in my casket to see that." She sprayed three whiffs of something that smelled like mixture of gardenias and Kentucky bourbon around her neck and dropped the bottle into her purse. "Just leave your luggage at the door. That's what bellhops are for, and they love taking care of little old ladies. I heard you talking to someone. Everything all right at home?"

"Fine and dandy." It wasn't, but I trusted Evie and John to handle things.

———•———

Sunday afternoon
Cedar Falls

Kate

We stopped for burgers after church. I took off my coat and was headed up to my room when I heard Daddy call me. "Kate, I need to ask you something before you go upstairs." I turned around and met Daddy in the hallway. He sent Chesler up to his room, took my hand, and led me to the kitchen.

"Have a seat, Katy J." He only called me Katy J when he was serious and was trying not to be. He started opening cans of beans to make the chili like what he was about to say was no big deal. "Got to get this chili going. I didn't get around to it last night."

"It won't be as good." I had a feeling about what was coming.

"It'll be fine. Nobody will know except us." He turned around and looked me straight in the face. "So tell me. What is this about the guest you've invited for our family Christmas?"

"You don't have to worry. He's not coming. Said he had other places to go."

"I wish he would come. I'd like to meet him. And tell me, when did you see this Mister Josh?"

"When I went to the woods yesterday, he was out walking, and I talked to him."

"Are you sure you just didn't make this up to try to get Granny Grace to come home early?" He started slicing onions.

"No, he's real. I did see him. He was whistling "I Wonder As I Wander," and I thought it was you. We talked about Aunt Susannah and Cecil and Sugar and about the holly and pine I was cutting. He looked the same. I didn't make it up Daddy. Just like the other times I've seen him. He's real."

"I know he's real to you, Kate, but can you understand how all this sounds to me and to your granny when you're the only one who ever sees him?"

"Then don't believe me. But I can take you to the spot and prove he was there."

Daddy washed his hands and came over to the table. "What do you mean you can prove it?"

"I was explaining to Mister Josh what Mama taught me about the meanings of the different trees. I gave him a juniper seed. He looked at it and said there was a whole forest in that little seed. Then he moved some leaves with his shoe, dropped the seed on the ground, and covered it with the leaves again. I can take you to the spot."

"Kate, this seed business is a bit farfetched and doesn't prove anything. Just how many juniper seeds do you suppose are on the ground out there in those woods?"

"Lots and lots, but only one squished one in that spot. I squished the berry to show him the seed. I can take you there."

"I think I'll pass on that, and I don't think Mister Josh will be coming to spend Christmas with us either. And no more saying things like that to Granny. She'll just worry about you. Is that what you really want?"

"No, sir. But I did see him, and I did invite him." I stood up.

"Go on up and change. Your Uncle Matt will be here in a bit, and you know Harry will want you to read to him if Matt brings him. Or maybe he can read to you. He's getting good at that now."

"Yes, sir." I didn't know how to make Daddy believe me if I couldn't take him to the woods and show him. I went to my room and changed into my jeans and sweater. The smell of chili was coming up the stairs when I heard the doorbell ring. I went downstairs and was glad to see Uncle Matt hadn't brought Harry. Reading to a five-year old was nothing I was interested in today.

"Hi, Uncle Matt. Evie's in the darkroom, but I can make you a cup of tea if you like." I followed him and Daddy to the kitchen.

"Actually, I think I'll pass. We had lunch with Mrs. Bell today, and she served a Christmas feast."

Daddy kept walking through the kitchen to the mud-room, "Matt, I'm going to the garage to get the metal box. It's cold out there, and we can look at the coins right here on the kitchen table."

I walked with Uncle Matt through the kitchen. "You really got me to thinking with your sermon this morning. I didn't know that Mary was so young. She wasn't much older than I am. And then I wondered about the angel telling her she was going to have God's Son. That must have been really scary. What would have happened if Mary refused?"

Uncle Matt sat down at the kitchen table. "Kate, you have never been short of good questions. And that's a really good one."

"So, what's the answer?"

"You know, Kate, God really does know what He's

doing. I think He knew Mary inside and out, and that's why He chose her. He knew she wouldn't refuse and that she would be a good mother for His Son."

Chesler came running down the stairs at the same time Daddy returned to the kitchen with the metal box. "Hey, Uncle Matt. I dug up a treasure. Granny said I could have it, so it's mine."

Daddy put the box down on the table in front of Uncle Matt. "This is how it was when I opened it." He turned to Chesler. "Ches, you need to stop thinking that. This was found in Granny's barn, so it's hers."

Chesler sat down next to Uncle Matt. "But Granny said I could have it."

"That's before she knew what was in the box, and I'm not certain she was thinking about what was possibly there when she said you could have it."

Chesler wasn't about to give up. "But she still said it, and Granny says it's a sin to fib."

Uncle Matt opened the metal box and kept unwrapping until he reached the coins. He removed the coins from the smaller box and laid them carefully on the table. "John, get me a bowl of warm, soapy water and a small towel. Kate, I left my bag on the table at the front door. There's a book in there about coins and a magnifying glass. Would you get them, please?" He was passing out orders like a surgeon about to operate.

I was back in time to watch Uncle Matt put one coin in the bowl of hot water and swish it around with his fingers. He brought it out and dried it carefully with the hand towel. "If this doesn't work, we'll try some vinegar. But let's hope this does it."

Nobody said a word.

He held the gold coin to the light and picked up the magnifying glass. "Hmm. Interesting." He turned it over and looked at the other side. "Very interesting."

Daddy was growing impatient like he did when I was telling him something and I took too long. "Just how interesting, Matt? Do you know what they are?"

"I think I do, and if these coins are what I think they are, this could get really interesting." He washed another one. "Same date and imprint." He looked up. "How many of these do you have?"

Chesler started counting out loud, but before he got to five, Daddy said, "Eighteen."

"Kate, hand me the book." Uncle Matt put the coin down and opened the book and started flipping pages. Even Chesler was quiet, like we were holding our breath. Uncle Matt placed the coin next to a picture. "Even more interesting. And you found these buried in Grace's barn?"

Daddy answered, "Yes, in the old part of the barn that Joseph didn't tear down. Grace says that barn is more than a hundred years old. Could be older. I thought some ancestor might have buried it during the Civil War."

"Probably a good assumption." Uncle Matt put the coin down and looked up. "These are all Indian Princess Head three-dollar gold pieces minted in 1854, and it looks like they were minted in Dahlonega, which makes them extremely rare. And the best I can tell, they're in mint condition, probably because they were uncirculated, and that makes them even more valuable. We need to find a professional to give us a better idea." Uncle Matt looked Daddy straight in the eye, "John, does anyone else know about these?"

"No. Well, just our family, and I did tell Granny about the box and coins, But I told her not to tell anyone. She promised, so she'll keep it to herself."

"Good. Now, do you have a safe-deposit box at the bank?"

I could tell Daddy was puzzled. "Yes, a small one. Not much of anything in it but some insurance papers."

"Put these in a smaller bag or box, and you take them straight to the bank in the morning. John, are you hearing what I'm saying? This is important. Before work, before whatever else you have planned, get these to the bank and into your safe-deposit box."

"Are they worth anything?"

"Yes. If they're what I think they are, they're worth a fortune. A large fortune."

Chapter Thirteen

———— ♦ ————

Monday morning, December 23
Cedar Falls

Kate

I looked at the clock beside my bed. Seven o'clock. If it were a school day, I'd just want to turn over and go back to sleep. But on days when I could sleep in, I was wide awake.

I got up, lifted the shade, and looked out my window to a curtain of gray clouds. There were snow drifts against the trunk of the elm tree and the shed out back. No redbird. The wind had howled all night, but it was calm this morning. A white Christmas for certain.

I put on my warmest robe and wool socks and went downstairs. I was quiet so I wouldn't wake Chesler. It was too early to deal with him. He would just be jumping up and down to go outside to play in the snow.

Evie was drinking coffee at the breakfast table, and Daddy was on the phone.

I went straight to the fridge for a glass of orange juice and sat down across from Evie. Usually when Daddy was on the phone this early, somebody had a problem. "Is somebody hurt? Does Daddy have to get out in the snow this morning?"

"No, sweetie, he's talking to Granny Grace."

"Is she okay?"

"Oh, yes. He was just checking with her about the Hortons. You slept through quite a bit of excitement last night. The good news is everyone is fine. John's just making some arrangements."

I turned to listen to what Daddy was saying. "Yes, Grace, I'll be leaving in just a few minutes, and I don't think there'll be a problem with the roads. No ice, just snow. Called in a favor, and my buddy Chris is clearing the lane as we speak. We'll make it work, and I know they'll be grateful." He paused. "And yes, as soon as the bank opens, I'll be putting the coins in my safe-deposit box until you get home. I'll check things out with Matt after Christmas. He was going to do more research."

Daddy hung up the phone and came to the table with his coffee. "Good morning, Kate. You need to eat a quick breakfast. I could use your help this morning."

I didn't really want to go anywhere today. I had plans to be lazy and to finish up a Christmas present for Baby Hank. "What's going on? What do I have to do?"

"I need to get back out to Granny's house, and I need you to go with me. It's been quite a night. And you, my sleepy-headed girl, missed the excitement for once in your life."

"What? What happened?"

"Evie made some hot oatmeal. Grab yourself a bowl, and hurry and get dressed. We need to get to the farm. I'll tell you on the way. I'm going to get dressed myself." He kissed Evie's cheek on the way out of the room. "I know you want to go to help," he said to her, "but I've rounded up a couple of the guys, and we'll make short order of this. You just stay here with Chesler and coordinate some things. Kate will help out. I'll let you know what's going on. Maybe you can go out later in the day."

Evie followed Daddy out of the kitchen. I was glad she left because I dumped that bowl of oatmeal in the garbage. It tasted like pasty cardboard and looked like wet chicken feed. It made my stomach churn. I knew it came out of one of those paper pouches instead of the good kind that came in a box that Mama cooked in apple juice with raisins and cinnamon. I made myself a peanut butter sandwich and ate it while I dressed. Maybe I shouldn't be worried since Daddy said everyone was fine, but I hated not knowing what had happened last night.

We weren't even out of the driveway before Daddy started his report. He knew I liked all the details. "Okay, here goes, so listen up. After you went to bed last night, Mrs. Horton called about Cecil. He left the house late in the afternoon after it started snowing and walked up the lane to Granny's to gather the eggs and check on the hens and the guineas before dark. He should have been back within an hour, but he didn't get home. She didn't know what to do, so she called me."

"Is Cecil hurt?"

"No, Cecil's fine, but it could have been bad. The wind was so fierce and the snow was blowing so hard he got disoriented on his way back home. He was smart, though, and retraced his steps to get back to the barn and stayed there to wait out the storm. When he didn't come home, Bonnie called, and I got a couple of the men from church to go and help me search. We went out there with our search lights to look for him. Snow drifts were piling up, and we couldn't drive from Granny's to the Hortons, so we looked for two hours on foot. We called out to him, but that wind was howling so bad, he couldn't have heard us. After two hours, we headed back to Granny's to call for more help. That's when I found Cecil in the barn."

"Why didn't you look there first?"

"I did. I looked around but saw no sign of him, so I didn't go in the barn. The strange thing was that when I got back, there were some footprints from Granny's house to the barn that weren't there before. That's what caused me to go out there to look, and there he was. We called his mom to let her know he was safe. I tried to get him to come home with me, but he wanted to go home. The snow was still blowing sideways, and the lane down to their house was too deep in snow to drive it, so I gave him a choice of coming here or staying at Granny's house."

"So, there were footprints?" I thought of Mister Josh, and I remembered how he had always shown up at the Hortons' last spring when they needed something. "Is Cecil at Granny's now?"

"He was, but it's not the end of the story. Cecil tromped through the snow at daybreak when it was light enough he could see. But when he got home, he discovered a mess. They had no power and a tree had fallen across the back porch and damaged the kitchen windows. That place isn't much more than a shack, and I'm surprised it didn't blow totally away last night. So Cecil walked back to Granny's and called me from her house to ask me to report the power outage."

"But they have a fireplace. I hope they stayed warm last night."

"Cecil built them a fire this morning." Daddy lowered his voice almost to a whisper. "You know, Kate. It was the strangest thing. When we got to the farm last night, I looked around the barn and saw no sign of Cecil. And yet those footprints were there when we got back. I'll be asking Cecil about that this morning. He's a fine and responsible young man. Had to become the man of the house with his daddy on the road driving a truck most of the time. Kind of like you becoming the woman of the house when your mama went to heaven. I'm proud of both of you, and I'm counting on your help this morning."

By the time Daddy finished his story, we were pulling into Granny's driveway. I was still thinking about those footprints. "So what am I doing here? What am I supposed to do to help? Chop wood? I'm not so good with power lines."

"No. We're going to need you to take care of Sugar and the baby for a little while. I called Granny this morning because I knew she would want to help. Her house is empty, and she has power, so we're moving the Hortons up here to Granny's. That's going to take a little doing this morning with Christmas, and they don't know how long they'll be staying here."

"So how are you getting down that road to their house?"

"Called in a favor from my buddy Chris, and he's already cleared the lane. I'll go down and get the kids and bring them to you. And then I'll go back to help Mrs. Horton load up what she needs to bring up here. It's Christmas, and we're bringing them and all their Christmas to Granny's house. So I need you to take care of Sugar and the baby while we get that done."

"Okay. I can do that." I was glad that Cecil and his family would have a warm place to be, and I knew Granny's house was probably the finest house they had ever seen. Mama and Granny Grace always said that everybody needs a somebody, and our job was to be the somebody, especially when it came to helping folks. I wanted to be the somebody to help the Hortons, but I really wanted to be the somebody celebrating Christmas at Granny's.

Guess Granny's house will have Christmas after all.

Monday morning
Old Edwards Inn

Granny Grace

I was late to the dining room for breakfast and took my seat next to Roger. The same breakfast waiter was Johnny-on-the-spot with a fresh cup of coffee, and I needed it this morning. Carl sat at the end of the table. "For goodness' sake, Grace, did somebody lick the red off your peppermint stick? Your face does not look like it's Christmas and that we're headed to a castle this morning."

"I really appreciate your duly-noted concern, Carl. And no, all the red is still on my peppermint stick." I put my napkin in my lap.

Henrietta piped in. "Well, you were on the phone when I left the room. Everything all right at home?"

"As all right as it can be. John called to tell me about the Hortons."

Lottie asked, "Is that the family that lives down the dirt road from you? The one we did the painting and sewing for?"

I took a sip of coffee. "The same. Troubles just seem to hover over that poor family. John said the wind was something else last night, and it knocked out the power to their house, and some falling trees did damage to their back porch and kitchen windows. Mr. Horton is on the road trying to get home for Christmas."

Lottie patted my hand. "So, what time are they moving into your house, Grace?"

I looked at her. "Well, pray tell, how did you know that?"

Lottie answered, "I didn't know *that*. I just know you." Everybody at the table chuckled. "Grace, remember when you led our little group of ladies last spring to vandalize the church to get their attention about helping poor folks in the community?" I pushed my chair back a little. "So, now I'm the one getting blamed for that."

Roger spoke. "Grace, we're not talking about blame here. We're talking about credit. Everybody in Cedar Falls knows how you are about helping folks, and Lottie just knew that you would tell John to bring them to your house."

Lottie added, "That's right, Grace. I was just trying to pay you a compliment. Why, you brought about more excitement in town vandalizing the church than we've had since the courthouse burned down and they were looking for the arsonist."

Carl snickered. "Yeah, you gals were something else. And smart, I might add. Nobody suspects sweet little old ladies of anything, especially something like that."

Henrietta swiped Carl with her napkin. "Sweet little old ladies, you say? Sounds like you don't know much about these little old ladies, and it sounds like we'd better change the subject so that you don't accidentally get left when the van pulls off."

I agreed with Henrietta. "Good idea. John is helping the Hortons move into my house as I speak. Looks like my lonely old house is going to be full for Christmas after all."

Roger nudged me with his elbow. "Don't you go worrying about the Hortons, Grace. When we get home, Carl and I'll get a few of the guys together, and we'll go out and get the Hortons' place all fixed up. It'll be good as new."

We finished our breakfast and loaded the van. Carl took the pilot's seat to help Roger navigate. Roger announced,

"Okay, we're about to be on our way. I've checked on road conditions, and we should be safe to travel, and I'm thinking we should arrive around two o'clock. Put on your seatbelts and get comfortable, and Carl, play that Perry Como music. We need a little Christmas this morning."

Henrietta had had one too many cups of coffee this morning. Her On button was stuck, and she didn't even take a breath between stories. After a half an hour of her going full steam, I leaned my head back and closed my eyes. I hoped that would shut her up. She was beginning to sound like my guinea, Sadie, and just as annoying. My traveling buddies were good folks, but I was used to my peace and quiet.

And I haven't had much of that since I left home.

I was thinking about the castle we were headed to. Henrietta had showed us the pictures again this morning at the breakfast table and reminded us we'd be spending Christmas in luxury—like something out of a fairytale, she said. Then I thought about the Hortons and my own family, and how John was stepping in to help. I imagined that he and Evie and Susannah Hope would see to it that the Hortons had a Christmas tree and plenty of groceries. And maybe Kate would remember what we taught her about being the somebody. Being that somebody just might get rid of her mullygrubs and help her to have a real Christmas.

Chapter Fourteen

———— ◆ ————

Monday morning
Cedar Falls

Kate

I held the sleeping baby and followed Sugar around while she walked through Granny Grace's house. She held her little hands behind her back and didn't touch a thing. She looked at me with her big brown eyes. "Kate, we get to stay here for Christmas? For real, we get to stay in this house?"

"Yes, you do. My daddy has gone back to your house to help your mom get your clothes and the Christmas presents and everything you need to stay here for a few days. My Granny is on a trip, and you and your family will spend Christmas right here. You can watch television and have your own room. And I can tell you Christmas is great in this house. We always had Christmas Eve right here in this room." I heard the back door slam. "Look, Sugar, here comes your mom."

Daddy was right behind Mrs. Horton, carrying a couple of boxes, and Cecil followed with two more. Daddy led Mrs. Horton to the guest bedroom and put her box of clothes on the bed. Then he took the other box and told Cecil to follow him. He took them down the hall to the bunk room, the bedroom Granny Grace had planned for all her grandchildren. "Cecil, you and Sugar can stay in here. I'll put your things over here on this bunk."

"But Daddy, I told Sugar she could have her own room. Please, can she sleep in the guest room with all the quilts?"

Daddy looked at Sugar. "That's where her parents will be sleeping. But Sugar, I think you'll love the bunk room. That's the room Granny made special for Kate and Chesler and Baby Hank."

"I think I will. I've never slept in a room all by myself anyway."

I helped Sugar get her clothes out of the box and showed her around the room and all the things Granny and Mama had made. Then I heard Daddy hollering, "Need some help in here."

When we got to the great room, Daddy was trying to hold a Christmas tree up in the corner. Cecil was on the floor doing something to the tree stand. It was a scrawny tree, not like Granny would have had. And it didn't have fancy Christmas decorations either. But it surely made Sugar happy when Cecil plugged in the lights.

I watched Sugar looking up at that Christmas tree and Mrs. Horton beside her, holding the baby. Mrs. Horton sounded like she was about to cry. "Mr. Harding, we sure do thank you for all you've done. You went out in the cold last night to find Cecil, and you brought us here this morning. Please let Mrs. O'Donnell know how grateful we are to have such a beautiful and warm place to stay. You are such good people. You've helped us so much. I hope to be able to repay you all one day."

Daddy walked over beside me. "No need for repayment. Everybody needs a little help sometimes. You and Cecil were helping Grace by watching the place while she's away. You two are just being neighborly." Daddy patted me on the head. "Well, we need to get back to town if there's nothing else you need."

I looked at the box on the sofa. "One more thing, Daddy. I see Christmas presents in that box on the sofa. Sugar, let's put those under the tree."

Before we left Granny Grace's house, it was full of Hortons and Christmas.

———•———

Monday night
The Kentucky Castle

Granny Grace

The drive to Lexington took longer than usual on account of the snow. I lost count of how many times I had heard "I Wonder As I Wander." I was doing plenty of wondering as I was wandering around away from home at Christmas all right.

Driving up to that gated entrance to the castle was like nothing I'd ever seen before. The staff met us at the door and invited us to have a slice of fig cake and coffee by the fireplace while they took care of our luggage. I was working hard to get rid of the gray cloud that had hovered over my head all day, and it helped when Henrietta announced we each had a private room for the next four nights. Seems the weather had caused cancellations, and we were the only ones here.

When everyone went to their rooms to rest for a while, I decided to take a look around before going up. People came from all over the country just to stay here, but I'd lived my whole life in these parts, and I'd never seen this place or anything like it. It was like something in one of those fancy magazines Susannah Hope was always looking at. Polished wood floors and a staircase that looked like some Hollywood movie star wearing a beaded gown might be coming down it any minute. Heavy drapes covered the windows. Wood-paneled walls, and more brass lighting fixtures than the White House.

I took the elevator up to my room on the second floor just because I could. I opened the door to fresh flowers, heavy curtains, satin bedding, and hand-carved wooden chairs that made the commode seat look comfortable. Susannah Hope would be perfectly happy here with acres of velveteen and lace and crystal lamps, but I'd rather be in my old chintz-covered chair at home and wrapped in my crocheted afghan and looking at acres of forest.

I dressed for dinner and even put on my jewelry. Henrietta had made sure I left my barn jacket and boots at home, but these few days made me real glad Sunday only came once a week. All this dressing up was not for the likes of me.

We met in the parlor at five o'clock as planned, all dressed up like we were meeting the queen of England. Henrietta had asked Rose to read us a Christmas story before dinner. She had obviously practiced reading it at home. I guessed she missed reading the Christmas stories to the children at the library and was giving us the story at full throttle. All her drama would have been downright comical if she hadn't been trying so hard.

Dinner was served at five-thirty, and Henrietta put me next to Roger again. I hadn't seen that many forks and spoons on one table since we sorted the new silverware in the church kitchen. There were a humpteen brass candlesticks with red candles and a bowl of red roses and holly right in the center of the table, and the meal was five-star.

The Christmas Portrait Surprise

Prime rib and fancy vegetables, and lane cake for dessert. The table conversation was lively with reports of everyone's room furnishings, but I stopped listening when I noticed the tablecloth—white Battenburg lace, starched and ironed without one spot on it to indicate anyone had ever had a gravy-sopping meal on it. Not like our family tablecloth for Christmas.

All the conversation and the stringed quartet playing "I Wonder As I Wander" just became background noise when I began to hear Kate's voice in my head. "Granny, you're right. You can't take the chocolate back out of the hot chocolate, but you sure can pour it all down the drain, and that's what you're doing leaving your family at Christmas."

What am I doing here? Is Kate right? Maybe I'm needed at home. Especially now with the Hortons.

Then I noticed the heavy, burgundy velveteen drapes drawn to cover the windows on the west wall of the dining room, and I could hear Joseph. *"We're finished with draperies and pulling shades. Windows were made to look through, and we're going to enjoy looking through all our windows. We'll just wait for the Good Lord to pull down the night sky over the sunset."*

That haunting melody about wondering and wandering would not go away. I had been teetering on the edge of some serious mullygrubs all day, but a sudden, deep sadness smothered me, snuffing out what little joy I had, like those velveteen curtains squelching the sunset. I excused myself from the table and walked across the dining room. The faint melody of "I'll Be Home for Christmas" from a single violin accompanied the drama in the deepest part of my being. Somebody would be home for Christmas, but it wouldn't be me.

I approached the window and pulled the dark drape to one side. There sat a redbird on a snow-covered cedar branch, twitching its head back and forth like it was asking me a question. Then I asked myself the question I'd been afraid to ask since we loaded the van Friday morning. *What in the world am I doing? Maybe Kate was right, and I am just being selfish. Diana Joy's gone. Joseph's gone. But I'm still here, and I chose to be gone. I know it's the sunset time of my life, but I'm no Indian squaw crawling off somewhere to die. And I have grandchildren who will miss me this Christmas.*

The redbird flew, and that's when I saw the brilliant sunset, shellacked across the sky just for me, just like it would be at home. *There's still light; there's still color. I've just pulled the shade so I wouldn't have to see it all fade away.*

My sadness melted and disappeared in that sunset. I wanted to sing or shout or do something to let somebody know I was still alive. *I've steeped my whole life in my family, and I'll not spend another minute drowning in this tank of nonsense. Now's not the time to pull the shade on Christmas. I'll wait and let the Good Lord do that in His own time. I'm going home.*

Without further ado, I made my apologies to my friends at the table and told them I was needed at home. Then, leaving behind the murmur of surprised responses, I marched myself to the front desk and asked that skinny little clerk to find me a driver that would get me to Cedar Falls tonight. He wasn't sure he could find someone who'd be willing to make the drive in the snow, but I told him I'd pay whatever it took. I'd been a practical woman all my life, but now was not the time for practical.

My friends knew there was no use in trying to talk me into staying, so they stood and waved as I departed. Three hours later, I was sitting in front of my fireplace with Bonnie, sipping chamomile tea, and giggling about what my family would say if they'd seen me, dressed in a sparkly sweater, getting out of the white stretch limo in my driveway tonight.

The Christmas Portrait Surprise

I dialed John's number. "I know it's late, John, but put Kate and Chesler on the phone, please." I waited. "Kate, I'm home. I'm back here at the farm sipping tea with Bonnie." I heard happy squealing. "Got to thinking about my smart granddaughter who knows it's a shame to pour good hot chocolate down the drain. So if you don't have something planned for tomorrow, how about coming out to help me and Bonnie with the onion soup, and we'll get a head start on the Christmas-morning cinnamon buns?"

I hadn't heard that kind of excitement in Katherine Joy's voice in a long time. "I will, Granny Grace. Daddy'll bring me. I know he will."

I listened to her muffled conversation with John. I couldn't tell exactly what they were saying, but I knew happy sounds when I heard them.

"Granny, Daddy said he'll bring me in the morning."

"Good, I'll get out an extra apron. Goodnight, sweet girl."

I was about to hang up when I heard Kate speak again. "Wait, Granny. I'm really glad you're home where you ought to be. And what about the Christmas tablecloth? You want me to bring it in the morning?"

"No need for that. That tablecloth is yours, Katherine Joy, for your Christmas table. We're starting this Christmas with a brand-new one."

Chapter Fifteen

---◆---

Tuesday morning, December 24
Cedar Falls

Granny Grace

$\mathcal{I}$ missed my chance to sleep in a castle, but waking up at the farmhouse had never felt better. I didn't have to pull the curtains or lift the shades to see the sunrise. And my jeans, sweater, and boots felt so good. I was home.

Bonnie was already up and had a fire going when I walked into the kitchen. "Good morning, Bonnie."

"And good morning to you, Grace. I just made the coffee. I hope you rested well in your own bed."

"Yes, I did. No place I'd rather be. Not even a castle. And I couldn't be happier that you're here too." I caught myself. "Well, I didn't exactly say that right, did I? I'm awfully sorry about your house, but I am glad you and the children are here this morning."

"Only because you're the kindest person I've ever known, Grace. You have been the best neighbor anyone could ever have."

"Thank you, Bonnie. But that's what we're all supposed to be—good neighbors. I could get used to waking up with a fire going and fresh coffee. Thank you." I poured myself a cup and sat down to the table. "I'll stir us up some biscuits and bacon and eggs after I've had my first cup. But let's talk about the day."

Bonnie joined me with her coffee. "I'll help with breakfast or anything else you need. I'm just grateful the children are safe and warm. I brought the groceries I had purchased for Christmas, and they're in the fridge. We don't want to be any kind of burden or bother to you. So, I'll do whatever you say today. I don't know when the power will be back on at the house. Maybe we won't be a bother for too long."

"Please don't consider yourself a bother. I don't. From what I hear, there's a bit of damage to the kitchen windows, and John's already taken care of what he could. In fact, he and Kate will be walking through the door any minute. But I don't think you should count on the power or the kitchen to be repaired until later in the week, so let's just sit here and plan ourselves a nice Christmas."

"A nice Christmas? I had hoped it would be."

"It will be. We have so much to celebrate. I could use your help today. Susannah's sending out the groceries we need to make Christmas Eve dinner for your family and ours. John's bringing it all this morning. We have a few traditions around here, and Christmas Eve at the farm is one of them. We'll have our early supper of French onion soup, grilled cheese sandwiches, Waldorf salad, and lots of sweet treats before we go to the Christmas Eve service. And we want you to go with us. Will your husband be home in time for supper and church?"

I couldn't help noticing the smile on her face when I mentioned her husband coming home. "Yes, he will. He should be home by early afternoon."

"Now, after the service tonight, I'll be going home with John and his family, and you'll have the farmhouse to yourself this evening and tomorrow morning for your family Christmas while we have ours in town at John's house. I have to make the rounds to see my grandchildren on Christmas morning. I'll do some cooking at John's, and Susannah Hope is already cooking up stuff for Christmas lunch. Maybe you can do a little cooking yourself to add to the table. Then we'll all come out here for our family Christmas feast for lunch about one o'clock. How does that sound to you?"

"Are you sure about us being here for Christmas with your family?"

"About as sure as I am that Christmas is the best day of the year. We'll all be family together. Now, our bunch is loud and little bit crazy, but the food is the best."

"Grace, I would like that very much. I know my family would like it too. I'll start cooking this afternoon."

"Sounds good. Nothing like a good plan." I got up and looked out the window above the sink. "Well, they're here. Oh, and Chesler's with them, so our quiet, peaceful morning is over."

Kate and Chesler met me at the back door with big hugs. When they finally turned me loose, I twirled around with my arms spread. "Look, Chesler, I'm alive. Not ready for the old Indian burial ground yet. It's Christmas, and I'm home, and we're going to have the best Christmas you can imagine."

I felt his little arms go around me again. "Yeah, Granny. Now it'll really be Christmas."

John put down bags of groceries on the table and spoke to Bonnie. "You could feed all the fellows at the fire department with all these groceries, but Susannah said you needed them. Cecil up yet? If he is, I'd surely like to have a little talk with him."

"He should be ready shortly. I woke him and Sugar and asked them to get dressed and straighten their room."

The Christmas Portrait Surprise

Bonnie hesitated. "It's okay, Mr. Harding, if you give him a good talking to about Sunday night. I know that he caused lots of trouble, and you and your friends put yourselves in danger to find him."

"I plan to give him a good talking to all right. I plan to tell him he's about the bravest, wisest, most responsible adolescent I know." John looked at Kate. "Well, maybe except for Katy J over there. She's pretty responsible and just a little on the bossy side too."

"You stop talking about my favorite granddaughter that way, John." I put my arm around Kate's shoulders.

She looked up and said, "You know, Granny, you might not be able to say that anymore if Aunt Susannah Hope's baby is a girl. Then I won't be your favorite and only granddaughter."

Cecil walked in shyly with Sugar right behind him. They were well-mannered kids, and I was proud of Bonnie for doing such a good job with them. I knew it hadn't been easy. "Good morning, you two. Now we can have ourselves some breakfast." I looked at John and Kate. "Have you had breakfast?"

John nodded yes, and Kate shook her head no. "Okay, I'll make a whole pan of biscuits. There'll be plenty for everybody with some left for Sadie. Just have a seat at the table. John, get yourself some coffee. Kate, pour Sugar and Cecil a glass of milk, and help me get all these groceries put away."

Kate had always been a willing helper, but she seemed even more eager this morning. Seeing her sweet face, looking more and more like her mama's, was convincing enough that I'd made the right decision.

Bonnie went to check on the baby. John sat down at the head of the table near Cecil, and I started rattling pans and bowls and jars of homemade jelly.

———•———

Kate

I knew I needed to help Granny with breakfast, but I was more interested in what Daddy was asking Cecil. I saw Cecil shake his head, and then I heard Daddy tell him how brave he was and how responsible he was in taking care of his family and himself during a snowstorm. I started setting the table so I could hear them better.

Cecil did like he always did at school—he hung his head, and his cheeks turned red.

Daddy said, "And then leaving early in the morning and going home to check on your family. Gathering the wood to build the fire to get them warm until we could get everyone over here. You're turning into a fine and responsible young man, Cecil."

Cecil sounded like he did when the teacher asked him a question. No emotion, just a plain, straight answer. "I didn't gather the wood, sir. It was already on the front porch."

"That just means you knew the storm was coming and planned ahead. You gathered it to be ready."

"No, sir. I mean I did gather some wood Sunday before the storm blew in, but I put it on the back porch. Since the tree crashed onto the back porch roof, I couldn't get to the wood I put there. Sugar said there was wood on the front porch. She said some old man stacked it up on the porch after I left to come check on the chickens Sunday afternoon. I didn't believe her, but I looked, and the wood was there just like she said."

I knew it was Mister Josh, just like I had seen him deliver grocery bags to the Hortons' front porch last spring. I'd been out in the forest taking pictures of the wood violets and ferns when I saw him. I tried to take his picture, but he was just gone.

I joined the conversation. "Did Sugar say what this old man looked like?"

"Said he was old with kinda long gray hair sticking out from under his wool cap. He had on a coat and gloves. She said he stacked the wood and waved at her through the window and left." Cecil looked at Daddy. "Sugar makes up stuff sometimes, but all I can say is the wood was there."

Daddy shook his head. "Well, it's a good thing it was. I want to ask you about something else. I've been thinking, and I can't quite figure this out. When we first got here Sunday night to search for you, I looked around the outside of the house and down the path to the barn, but I didn't see any sign of you. But the thing is this: when we came back to the farmhouse to call for more help, I saw tracks that were not here when we first got here. They were deep, fresh tracks from the house out to the barn. Could they have been yours?"

Cecil gave his straight answer just like he always did at school. "No, sir. They could not. When I realized I couldn't be sure to get home because the wind and snow blinded me, I followed my tracks back to the barn so I wouldn't get lost. My plan was to wait the storm out in the barn. That's what I was doing when you found me."

Daddy was running his fingers through his hair like he did sometimes when he was trying to figure something out. "So now, Cecil, it's okay if they were your tracks, but you're certain they weren't?"

"I'm certain, sir. I didn't come near the house. And besides, I got back to the barn about seven thirty. I used some old blankets I found and a tarp to stay warm. I turned off my flashlight to conserve the battery until I really needed it. Sir, you didn't find me until after midnight. Even if I had made the tracks, snow would have covered them by then."

"You're right, son. The snow was coming down pretty thick, and the wind was blowing sideways. Maybe I just thought I saw tracks. But something led me to that barn, and that's how I found you."

I couldn't be quiet any longer. "It was Mister Josh."

I felt Daddy's eyes and Granny's eyes zero in on me like I mighta just said there was no Santa Claus.

Granny was the first to ask, "And what makes you think it was Mister Josh?"

Cecil looked up. He knew.

"Because that's what Mister Josh does. He just shows up, does something, and then he leaves. I saw him in the woods at our house Saturday, and I saw him at the Hortons when I was taking pictures of the wildflowers at Easter. He's real, and I bet . . ."

When I said that word, I knew it would get a rise out of Granny. "So now my granddaughter has started betting."

"No, ma'am. I didn't mean that exactly. It's just that I know it was Mister Josh. He's real." I looked at Cecil for support. "What do you think, Cecil? Have you met him?"

"Once."

"You think it could have been Mister Josh who delivered the wood and helped my daddy find you?"

Cecil shrugged his shoulders and looked at me. "Maybe."

Granny washed her hands and dried them on her apron. "Enough about that. We may never know, but what we do know is that we're all here safe and sound on Christmas Eve and the biscuits are ready to come out of the oven. Let's have some breakfast and get ready to celebrate our Lord's birth this evening."

I looked at Cecil. He had a shy grin on his face, but he looked me straight in the eye and gave me the thumbs-up sign.

Chapter Sixteen

————— ♦ —————

Christmas Day
Cedar Falls

Kate

$\mathcal{I}$ pulled the covers up and turned over to look out the window. That sky was as black as chimney soot this morning and sparkling with stars. The clock on my bedside table said five twenty-three—too early to get up, even on Christmas morning. Granny's breathing sounded like a cat purring. All that time I'd been sad and angry she wouldn't be here for Christmas, and here she was next to me for the first ever Christmas Eve sleepover.

My stirring must have roused Granny. "Kate?" she whispered. "You awake?"

I rolled over onto my back. "Kinda. It's early."

I felt Granny Grace's hand stroking my hair. "Not too early to get up and get started celebrating Jesus's birthday."

"Granny, you've never been at our house early on Christmas morning. We celebrated Jesus last night at the Christmas Eve service, but I can tell you Chesler will be looking for Santa Claus the minute his eyes are open. Then we can think about Jesus again."

Granny chuckled. "Something tells me you're right about that. I need to get myself ready for the day and get the cinnamon buns in the oven. Susannah Hope and Don and Baby Hank will be here about eight thirty to open presents, and then I'll need to get on to the farm by ten. Lots of cooking to do today."

"I can go with you to help."

"I'll take you up on that. We'll have some new feet under our Christmas table today. It's a good thing I have a brand-new Christmas tablecloth." Granny sat up in the bed and stretched like a cat. "Let's go, girl. Let's wake up some people and start the fun."

No more sleeping in this house with Granny up and Christmas on her mind. She was dressed before me and had her hair balled up like she always wore it. She straightened her collar. "No day to be wandering around in your bathrobe."

She didn't have to push me to get up. I jumped out of bed, put on my Christmas sweater and jeans, and brushed my hair.

Granny yelled, "Merry Christmas," when she walked into the hall and strutted through the house singing "Joy to the World." I feared she woke the neighbors, she was singing so loud. She went straight to the kitchen to make coffee and preheat the oven for the cinnamon buns.

Chesler came running down the stairs in his pajamas and sock feet like Sadie was chasing him. He went straight for the Christmas tree just like I knew he would. Daddy and Evie joined us in the living room after they'd poured themselves a cup of coffee.

Wrapping paper started flying when Chesler found all the boxes with his name on them. So many presents, and we all got what we wanted. I figured Evie saw to it that Chesler and I got everything on our list.

The Christmas Portrait Surprise

We saved the other family gifts to open when Aunt Susannah Hope got here. I helped straighten up the living room while Granny was busy in the kitchen and the rest of them were getting ready for the day.

The smell of Granny's cinnamon buns in the oven was the best thing I'd ever smelled in my whole life. I remembered how Mama and Grandpa loved those buns and hot chocolate on Christmas morning. And I was grateful Granny was home, and I was even grateful Evie was family now.

At eight thirty on the dot, just because she's like that, Aunt Susannah Hope and her brood walked through the front door. Uncle Don carried bags of gifts, and she had a tray of cookies and held on to Baby Hank like he might escape if she let him go.

After the cinnamon buns and real hot chocolate, we gathered in the living room to open our presents and for the reading of the Christmas story. There was a lot of oohing and ahhing in that room when we opened our gifts.

When the floor was covered in Christmas paper for the second time that morning and there were no more boxes under the tree, Daddy stood. But I saw that he didn't have his big Bible like he always did. "It's Christmas morning again, and you know we have some traditions, and one of them is reading the Christmas story. That was always Grandpa Joseph's job until he went to heaven, and then it became my job. But we're starting a new tradition today. As you know, Chesler has learned to read, and I've asked him to read us the Christmas story from his favorite Bible story book. I thought Baby Hank might really like that. Ches, you ready?"

"Yes, sir."

I wished Mama could have seen Chesler, standing there in his Star Wars pajamas and sock feet with his curly red hair like hers going in every direction. She woulda been so proud. He didn't wiggle, and he never stumbled on a word. While he was reading, I looked around the room, and everybody had looks on their faces like they were happy and a little sad at the same time. Daddy was right about Baby Hank. He sat still in Uncle Don's lap and listened. When Chesler finished, everybody clapped—maybe because Baby Jesus was born or maybe because Chesler did such a good job. Daddy said it was time to pray, and he asked Uncle Don to thank God for Jesus and that our family was together.

I looked at Granny Grace before I bowed my head. She nodded toward the window behind the Christmas tree and winked. There was the redbird perched in the cedar tree peeping into our house on Christmas morning. I looked back at Granny, and I think she had a tear in her eye like I did. Granny had said one time that Mama left her soulprint on all of us, and she had. Mama would always be a part of our Christmas, and there would always be a redbird to remind me of her.

Uncle Don had barely said "Amen" when Evie stood up. "Just one more thing. First, I want to say how grateful I am to be a part of this family. I love the traditions that you and Diana Joy started, because I have none. They are beautiful. Now, please don't laugh when I say this. I know I'm not very good at many of the things the women in this family are good at. But I love each one of you, and if it's okay, I have a tradition I would like to start."

Evie reached behind her chair and pulled out a large frame. When she turned it around so we could see, we were looking at a map of the world. "You know I'm not good at cooking and sewing and grocery shopping and the things that make for everyday family living, and I know that this whole family is exceptionally good about making gifts.

That's another thing I'm not good at, but I'm good at traveling and taking pictures and making memories. And this year, to start a new tradition, I want to give our family a memory-making journey. For the next six months until we start the journey in June, we'll have fun planning every detail to someplace special."

Evie turned to Granny. "And Grace, I know you're probably not excited about planning another trip right now, but I've made your reservations to go with us. If you look at this map, there is a gold star almost in the middle. Our very first family trip will be to—"

Granny Grace gasped. "Ireland? We're going to Ireland? I always, always wanted to go there. I'm going to give that Blarney Stone the biggest kiss it ever had."

Everybody laughed, and Evie answered, "I guess that means you will go with us. And yes, we're going to Ireland, the birthplace of the O'Donnell clan. Our first family trip will be to a place where we speak the language. And Grace, you'll finally get to spend the night in a castle, a real castle."

Evie looked at Daddy, "And John, I hope that someday years and years from now when we bring out this framed map on Christmas morning to see where we're going next, it will be covered in gold stars of all the places we've been, and we'll sit and remember all the sweet times we've had."

I knew the streak down my forehead was bright red, but not because I was mad or fibbing. It was because I was so happy. I couldn't believe it. We got to keep all our traditions, and Evie was starting a new one that we could look forward to forever. I was so glad she wanted Granny to go with us to Ireland.

Maybe Granny was right after all when she said it was good to make room for some new traditions. I knew I would always miss Mama at Christmas, but somehow, I thought I might learn to like Christmas again.

Evie set up her good camera and staged us all in front of the Christmas tree to take our family Christmas portrait because it was our tradition. Somehow I knew the redbird in the cedar tree would be in that picture.

We started packing up to go to Granny's, and I went to the dining room for the Christmas tablecloth. I brought it to Granny. "Shouldn't we take the Christmas tablecloth?"

"No need, sweet girl. I have one, remember? It's time to start a new one."

Granny was right. Once we all got to her place and sat down to eat, there were more feet under that long table than we had ever seen. The Hortons, Uncle Matt and his family, Uncle Luke and Aunt Lisa. And just when we were ready to get started, Granny made her announcement. "The table's full, but we have more coming."

I couldn't imagine who else might show up.

"Remember my traveling buddies that were taking the Christmas trip?" All eyes turned to Granny Grace. "Well, they'll all be here in about five minutes. Seems like I was either a bad or a mighty good influence on them. They decided they belonged in Cedar Falls and wanted to be a part of someone's family Christmas. I told them we were that family and there was plenty of love and food to go around." Granny laughed louder than I'd heard her laugh in a long time.

Uncle Matt stood up from the table. "Well, let's squeeze together, and make room for five more. And if you like, I can preach a Christmas sermon while we wait for their arrival."

Evie looked at her brother. "I have a better idea. Why don't we just sing a Christmas carol? Chesler, starting singing would you?"

When Granny's friends walked in, we were singing "O Come, All Ye Faithful." The singing stopped when Granny brought them to the table. She stood next to her friend, Miss Henrietta, and said, "Now, Henrietta, this is going to be a fabulous—a real fabulous—time." Then Granny prayed like God was right there just waiting. She thanked Him for the bounty on the table and the friends and family to share it. When she said, "Amen," the bowls and platters started their way around the table.

After we'd finished eating, Granny asked Evie and Aunt Susannah Hope to help clear the table and told everybody else not to move. I knew what was coming. Granny returned in a few minutes with my aunt and Evie, and they all had a fist full of red and green permanent markers. "Okay, this is how we do things at the O'Donnell Christmas table. Each of you will take a marker, sign your name, and put *1991* under your signature. If you want to write a little something, feel free. Just remember this tablecloth has to last us about thirty more Christmases."

After lunch, I saw Daddy, Granny, and Uncle Matt slip out to the sunroom. I didn't follow them, but I watched. Granny's face kept changing expressions, and finally she laughed so loud she had to sit down. Maybe they'd told her about the coins Chesler dug up in the barn, or maybe they'd told her a joke. I didn't care. I was glad to see Granny Grace home and so happy.

I walked to the dining room and just stood at the table. I was looking at all the signatures on the tablecloth when I felt Sugar's hand in mine. "Let me show you my name, Kate." She led me around to the other side of the table and pointed. "Mama wrote the numbers for me. I wanted to write something else, but I only know how to write my name."

"Tell me what you wanted to write, and I'll put it here above your name." I picked up a red marker from the china cabinet.

"I wanted to write 'I love Christmas at Granny Grace's house.'"

I looked down at Sugar, and her smile was bigger than the one on the ragdoll she got for Christmas. I wrote exactly what she said.

Christmas was different this year. Granny's house was full of folks and food and a whole lot of happy noise, and Evie clicked away to get everybody's picture. Our family Christmas portrait had turned into lots of Christmas portraits this year with the Hortons and all of Granny Grace's XYZ friends at our table. It was a Christmas of surprises no one expected—a real Christmas for me because Granny Grace was there, and she had a way of making everybody happy.

———•———

Granny Grace

The house was quiet again. Not an empty quiet but an all-is-well kind of quiet. All the family and friends had gone back home, and the Hortons were in bed. I was bone tired. A good tired like I had enjoyed myself all day and not the weary kind. The last embers of the fire that had been burning since early morning were calling my name, so I pulled my chair closer and threw the afghan over my legs. I needed a few quiet moments to savor the whole day.

Oh, I missed Joseph and Diana Joy, and Joseph would have loved seeing that dining room table he made with so many happy people around it. I wondered how he and Diana Joy might have been celebrating Christmas in heaven.

For my Christmas, there was no castle. No Indian burial ground. No magazine-perfect Christmas tree at the farmhouse. But oh, so much joy under this roof today. It would not have mattered how many times Henrietta said "fabulous"—nothing on the XYZ's trip compared with being at home with family and all our traditions for Christmas.

I sat for a while longer thinking about footprints in the snow, strawberry salad, Ireland, buried treasure in the barn and what I'd do with it, all the clicks of Evie's camera, and Chesler now reading the Christmas story. Nothing better than all that.

The fire was out, and I closed the screen. I walked by the dining room to look at the cloth on the table before turning out the kitchen light and going to bed. I read the signatures and saw what was written above Sugar's name.

And then I saw Kate's signature—*Katherine Joy Harding, 1991, Best Hot Chocolate Ever.*

Hot chocolate—good stuff all stirred together, and I didn't pour it down the drain after all. What she wrote wouldn't make much sense to anyone else, but it would forever be my and Kate's secret.

Epilogue

---◆---

Sixteen years later, Christmas 2007
Cedar Falls

Kate

$\mathcal{I}$ was home for Christmas again, where the family always gathered, and with the Christmas tablecloth. It would cover Daddy and Evie's table, and I couldn't wait for Granny to see what I had done. Everything would have been perfect, except Henry wasn't here.

One of the things Mama taught me was to embroider. Several years ago, Granny and I decided it would be a good idea to embroider over all those signatures and dates and notes to preserve them. Then I chose to embroider a border of holly around the hem and a redbird in the middle. I even embroidered a cup of hot chocolate next to my name for the Christmas of 1991. That was the Christmas when I'd learned about blending family and traditions.

It has taken years of tedious needlework, but my embroidery project was finished. The family Christmas tablecloth was preserved for at least another few decades until the stitching wore out. This would be the Christmas of its unveiling.

The Christmas Portrait Surprise

As was our tradition on Christmas Eve, we gathered for French onion soup, Granny Grace's famous grilled cheese sandwiches, and Waldorf salad, and then we went to church for the Christmas Eve service. Our family filled up the front two pews on the organ side. I was sad to think that I was surrounded by the people that I loved and Henry was alone at Christmas with strangers in some Ethiopian village.

Uncle Luke and Aunt Lisa were there with their three children. Aunt Susannah Hope and Uncle Don were there with Hank and Gracie. Uncle Matt was no longer the pastor at our church, but he and his family came to Cedar Falls to spend Christmas with us. We were their family now. The Harding bunch was there, and the Hortons and Laramie and her family were all seated behind us.

Chesler had skidded into town just in time for our dinner at Granny's and the church service. He was in veterinary school in Virginia and still single. When Granny told the pastor Chesler would be home for Christmas, the pastor asked him to sing. Chesler's singing at Christmas was a tradition everyone loved. Hearing his pure tenor voice brought back so many memories of Christmases past. I could hear Mama in his voice and see her in his red, curly hair.

I looked at his curls and remembered the silk bag with the lock of Mama's hair and the book of matches that Mister Josh had once left in my pocket when my plan to get Mama's Christmas present to heaven got me locked in the church on Christmas Eve after midnight. That had been my first encounter with Mister Josh. I'd seen and spoken with him a number of times since then, but he always seemed to vanish before anyone else saw him. But I always kept my eyes open for him, especially when I was home for Christmas.

The service was almost over with only the candle lighting and the singing of "Silent Night" left. The pastor was giving instructions when there was a bit of a ruckus at the end of the pew. I looked over, expecting it would be Chesler pulling one of his capers. But it wasn't. Instead, there was Henry, my precious Henry, stumbling his way down the pew to where I was. I hugged him like I was never letting him go. Henry was the best Christmas surprise.

Christmas Day was just like always with Granny's cinnamon buns and hot chocolate at the Harding house. We exchanged gifts, and we all waited for the arrival of the framed map. We laughed for almost an hour as we told stories of all those trips we had made. Evie's tradition had turned out to make more memories than we could have imagined. And the travel gave us a different perspective of the world. Lots of gold stars on that map, and Granny Grace had made every trip so far.

Finally, Evie brought out the map covered in gold stars, and there sat a large bright star just to the right of the center. "Well, we've been to Europe a few times," she said. "We've been to Africa and Asia and South America, and we have the pictures to prove it. But this summer we're all going to where this star shone brightly on the very first Christmas. We're going to Israel. And thanks to Granny Grace's generosity, all of us are invited to go, all eighteen of us in this room. It will be the journey of a lifetime and a rich experience to share with our family to walk where our Lord walked."

Granny Grace laughed out loud. "I want to thank Evie for letting me share in her Christmas tradition. And what she said is true! Every word of it. And I want to give Chesler a bit of credit for digging up an old metal box in the barn so we could afford to go. But another way of saying it is this: I'm getting a bit old to travel to all these exotic places, and I really enjoy staying at home these days. So I've decided this is going to be my last trip, and I trust you'll all behave without me in the future. But the Holy Land is where I want to go. And it would mean so much to me if you'd all go with me."

I sat between Henry and Chesler and squeezed their hands while Granny Grace was talking and remembered again that Christmas of 1991. It had had more than its share of surprises with Granny Grace's decision to take a trip and then unexpectedly coming home in a white limousine in time for Christmas. Then there was the snowstorm that practically destroyed the Hortons' house, and Cecil got stranded in Granny Grace's barn with unexplained footprints that led Daddy to find him. Our Christmas table had been full of folks that year—our family, the Hortons, and all of Granny's traveling friends showing up unexpectedly just in time for Christmas dinner. And then there was the metal box Chesler found.

That metal box. When Daddy and Uncle Matt told Granny on that Christmas Day the value of the coins in that box, she'd laughed so hard and so loud that she cried. Uncle Matt had taken the coins to a dealer to discover they were indeed three-dollar 1854 Indian Princess gold coins minted in Dahlonega. That made them rare. The fact they were uncirculated made them worth nearly two and a half million dollars. Granny had put the money to good use, taking care of her family and the needs of the poor in the community for the last sixteen years.

Lots of surprises had accompanied that Christmas of 1991, and this Christmas was no different. Henry's arrival was the best surprise I could have imagined. Seems our family Christmas portrait would have more unexpected surprises this year. And like Granny Grace always said, "Christmas is the season of surprises."

About the Author

 Phyllis Clark Nichols's character-driven Southern Fiction explores profound human questions using the imagined residents of small town communities you just know you've visited before. With a strong faith and love for nature, art, music, travel (especially sailing) and ordinary people, she tells redemptive tales of loss and recovery, estrangement and connection, longing and fulfillment ... often through surprisingly serendipitous events.

Phyllis grew up in the deep shade of magnolia trees in South Georgia. Born during a hurricane, she is no stranger to the winds of change. In addition to her life as a novelist, Phyllis is a seminary graduate, pianist, soloist, and cofounder of a national cable network with health and disability-related programming. Regardless of the role she's playing, Phyllis brings creativity and compelling storytelling.

She performs half-hour musical monologues that express her faith, joy, and thoughts about life—all with the homespun humor and gentility of a true Southern woman.

Phyllis currently serves on a number of nonprofit boards. She lives in the Texas Hill Country with her portrait artist, theologian husband.

Website: PhyllisClarkNichols.com
Facebook: facebook.com/Phyllis Clark Nichols
Twitter: twitter.com/PhyllisCNichols

Made in the USA
Coppell, TX
31 October 2021